MIDNIGHT BUTTERFLY

by

JOAN ELIZABETH LLOYD

CARROLL & GRAF PUBLISHERS, INC.

NEW YORK

Carroll & Graf Publishers, Inc.
A Division of Avalon Publishing Group
19 West 21st Street
New York, NY 10010-6805

ISBN: 0-7394-1054-7

Manufactured in the United States of America

CHAPTER 1

That makes tonight's winning lotto numbers 1, 2, 11, 13, 16, and 23. Good luck. And remember that if no one wins tonight, Saturday's New York State Lottery jackpot could be more than seventy million dollars."

Ellen Harold opened one of her green eyes, yawned, and glanced at the blue digits on the front of the VCR. Seeing that it was just after eleven, she realized that she had, as usual, fallen asleep in her lounge chair, watching a rerun of *Baywatch*. She yawned again and stared at the 11:00 P.M. news anchor, not really listening to the day's headlines.

Ten minutes later, as the anchorman introduced the sports reporter, Ellen swung her short legs off the chair and stumbled into the bathroom, scratching the back of her neck. Barely awake, she brushed her teeth and gazed into the mirror. She sleepily looked at her half-closed green eyes and her shoulder-length, baby-fine brown hair and slightly sunburned ivory skin. *Next time I mow the lawn*, she thought, *I've got to use more sun block.*

Didn't the guy say 13, 16, and 23? she thought as she entered her bedroom. *Hey, I might have at least three of the numbers.* Ellen played the local six-number lottery twice a week and always played the same numbers, 11 and 16 representing her birthday, 1 and 13, her older sister's, and 2 and 23, her late mother's. She scratched the back of her neck again, wondering whether three numbers pay off. She didn't really hear the rest but maybe she even had four. Afraid to hope, she undressed, pulled on her pajamas, and settled into bed. She closed her eyes and let herself drift, dreaming not of money but of romance.

She was tall, maybe five foot nine, slender. Men thought of her as willowy. Reed slim. She had thick auburn hair that fell in heavy waves almost to her waist. Tonight she was wearing an orange bathing suit like the women in Baywatch. She walked along a beach at sunset, the sand warm, the water cool as wavelets lapped at her dainty feet. Her blue eyes searched the strand before her, knowing the man she looked for would appear.

He looked a bit like David Hasslehoff, long, sandy hair dancing on his shoulders, tousled by the soft breeze. He had beautifully developed arms and shoulders, a hairless chest with well-defined layers of muscles. Muscles. She loved the idea of a man who could overpower her should he choose. But he wouldn't have to.

As they approached each other, he gazed at her, burning her with his stare, undressing her with his eyes. And she was more beautiful naked than she was in her suit. "You knew, didn't you?" he said when they were only a breath apart.

"I knew. When I first saw you, I knew." She reached out and flattened her palms against his warm skin. Beneath her hand she could feel the drumming of his heart.

"Now," he whispered. "Right now." He cupped her face, staring deeply into her eyes as his fingers glided past her temples to comb through her hair.

"Yes," she breathed.

His mouth descended and covered hers, his tongue playing beautiful melodies against her lips. She parted them, allowing his tongue entrance to her hidden cavern and the kiss lengthened until their universe was spinning out of control. She couldn't think, and knew she didn't want to, ever again.

Then, they were naked, lying on sand as soft as any feather bed, tiny waves playing with their toes. His hands covered her breasts, kneading her hot flesh, his mouth toying with her ears. "I want you," he murmured, "as I've never wanted anyone."

"Then take me," she replied, slipping her hands around his waist. Then he was inside her, his manhood large, filling every inch of her. His thrusts, his movements perfectly timed with her need, his huge body driving her upward, making her crave. His mouth covered her erect nipple, licking and sucking as his hips pressed his flesh more deeply into her.

"Oh, Lord," she said, "make me yours."

"You are mine," the man said, "always." And with one final push, warm fluid filled her and her pleasure was complete.

And in her bed, Ellen reached down and touched herself sleepily between her legs, enjoying the small spasms that completed her. Afterward, the transition from fantasy to sleep was smooth and she slept dreamlessly through the night.

The following morning, without getting out of bed, she pressed the button on top of her radio, hoping the local news would mention last evening's numbers. She had awakened thinking about the lottery and, from what she remembered from the previous evening, she probably had at least three of the numbers. The announcer's voice droned on. Suddenly, Ellen sat bolt upright and stared at the radio. "Last night's winning numbers were 1, 2, 11, 13, 16, and 23." *Those are my numbers,* she thought, pressing her hand against her breastbone, feeling the sudden pounding of her heart. *Those are my numbers. It can't be. Things like that just don't happen to people like me. I must have heard wrong.*

She threw on a pair of many-times-washed jeans and yanked on a navy T-shirt. Slipping her feet into sneakers without socks she ran out her door into the warm July morning. Without conscious thought she dashed around the corner to the little convenience store where she bought her ticket early every Wednesday and Saturday afternoon. Panting, she pushed through the front door. "Hi, Ellen," the counterman called in lightly accented English. "What brings you out this early?" Hispanic with deeply pigmented skin and heavy five o'clock shadow despite the early hour, his smile of obvious pleasure at seeing her exposed large white teeth.

"Hernando, do you have last night's winning lottery numbers?"

"Sure, they fax them to me so I can post them. Lemme see now." He shuffled some papers on the counter. "Yeah. Here they are: 1, 2, 11, 13, 16, and 23. You the big winner?" he asked with a grin. "Fifty million big ones. Cut me in, will ya?"

"Hey, Hernando," a voice called from the back room. "We just got another fax from the lottery administration.

Seems the only winning ticket for last night's jackpot was sold here."

Hernando turned to stare at Ellen but she barely noticed. She was in shock. Those were her numbers. Really. Hers. She fumbled in her jacket pocket and found her wallet. Inside was her ticket. She had to check that she had really bought the right numbers. But she had. Right? Her breathing sped up and her pulse raced and she could hear nothing but a buzzing in her ears.

She clutched the wallet as she became aware that Hernando was standing, staring at her. From the back room, the voice yelled, "I wonder who won all those bucks. Do we get to know?"

"I think we just might," Hernando yelled. "Are those really your numbers?" he asked Ellen. "I remember you told me once that you always play the same ones. Your family's birthdays. Right?"

Ellen stood with her wallet in her trembling hand, unwilling to open it and pull out the ticket. Maybe she had made a mistake and played the wrong numbers, but she always played the same ones. She should just look. "I can't," she whispered.

"Want me to look at your ticket for you?" Hernando asked.

Ellen nodded numbly and held out her wallet. Slowly Hernando took it in his huge hands, reached inside the bill compartment and withdrew the ticket. "Right date," he said as he studied the small slip of paper. He looked back and forth between the list and the ticket. "One, 2, 11, 13, 16, and 23. Holy shit. Those really are the numbers." He raised his eyes and again just stared at Ellen. "Holy shit, Ellen. Fifty million. Take it in a lump and you get maybe thirty-five. Pay half to the president, and some to the governor and you get to keep maybe fifteen or twenty. Holy shit. Twenty million smackers clear. Wanna buy this place? I can let you have it for only five million." His laugh was warm as he pounded Ellen on the back. "Wow!"

Unable to move, Ellen raked her numb fingers through her hair, reflexively tucking strands behind each ear, then scrubbed her eyes with her fists. She couldn't seem to keep from shaking. "You okay?" Hernando asked. "You want some water? Only ten bucks a glass." His booming voice filled the empty store.

She shook her head. She didn't want any water and she was definitely not okay. What was she? "I don't know," she mumbled. She took the ticket and her wallet from Hernando's hand. "What do I do now?"

"I can let lottery headquarters know but you might want to talk to a lawyer or an accountant first. What are you going to do with all that money?"

"I don't know," Ellen said, concentrating on putting the ticket back into her wallet. "I haven't a clue what I'm going to do," she muttered as she walked out of the store.

"I haven't a clue," Ellen said to her older sister on the phone a week later.

"Well, love," Micki said, "you don't need to make any decisions for a while." Micki, full-time mother of three school-aged daughters, had been talking to Ellen almost daily since Ellen had called and told her about the winning ticket. "As you know, my only advice is to be good to yourself."

"I know, but I don't know what that means." With advice from a local accountant she had claimed her prize the day after winning. She had enjoyed all the attention, the whirlwind ceremonies and TV appearances. She even had the picture of her with the giant check stuck in the corner of her bedroom mirror.

She had already put chunks of money in accounts for each of Micki's children and a sizable sum in a money-market fund for her sister and brother-in-law, over their loud objections. The accountant had introduced her to a broker who invested the rest of her money in certificates of deposit and conservative mutual funds. She now had an income of more than half a million dollars a year, but she hadn't any idea of what to do next. She was still getting tapes from the medical group she worked for doing data coding and typing up the required reports on her computer. She was still eating peanut butter sandwiches and Kraft macaroni and cheese and going out to the local Italian restaurant for spaghetti with meat sauce once or twice a week.

Nothing much had changed yet everything had changed. All the people in the neighborhood knew about her winnings. People she barely knew stopped her on the street with business propositions and she was constantly asked for contributions to aid the homeless, the needy, sick children, art museums, endangered species. Representatives of charities of all types wrote, called, and even rang her doorbell, anxious to help her spend her winnings. Several people named Harold had contacted her, sure they were long-lost relatives. "Micki, my sudden fame is driving me crazy. I got another dozen letters today from people and places I don't know, all wanting money. Yesterday Mrs. Cumberland, that wonderful grandmotherly type next door came over with a plate of fudge."

"That was nice of her." Micki hesitated. "Wasn't it?"

"I thought so, too, until she spent an hour telling me about her grandson who is the brightest mind since Einstein but can't afford college. You remember Randy Cumberland."

"Sure. He was a year after you in school. A bit dorky but sweet. College? He barely graduated from high school."

"Right. He's working at Ernie's gas station rebuilding engines, and he's perfectly content, right where he belongs, but his grandmother doesn't see it that way. When I talked to her about it, she insisted that the only reason he's not Phi Beta Kappa is money. My money."

"Oh shit."

"Everyone. Even Dr. Okamura went completely over the edge yesterday."

"Over the edge?"

"I went in to pick up my tapes and he came out of the back, all smarmy. Oily. He was all over me, smiling a big sticky-sweet smile. 'How's my favorite girl today?'

"How's my favorite girl? He's never said three words to me before. So I told him I was just fine and he leaned over, trapped me against his receptionist's desk and asked me out to dinner."

"He didn't," the voice through the phone gasped. "He's married, isn't he?"

Ellen tucked several strands of hair behind her ear and shifted the phone to the other side. "He did, and he's very married. Suddenly I'm the winner of the most-likely-to-make-a-man-cheat-on-his-wife contest. Yuck. I gently removed his arm from beside me and told him that I wasn't available."

"Do you think he knows about the money?"

"Why else? Come on, Micki. Be real. I'm not particularly attractive and he's never paid the least bit of attention to me before. It's all making me crazy. Everyone's changed."

"So get away. Move somewhere where no one knows you, and no one cares. You can go anywhere, you know."

"Yeah right. Take a cruise around the world. Live a frivolous life clipping coupons."

"Why not? You can certainly afford it."

Ellen propped the receiver between her ear and shoulder

and paced the length of her bedroom. "I couldn't do that. I couldn't just loll around. I'd have to do something."

"Okay. Go to medical school."

Ellen smiled. "Right."

"Listen, you can do anything you want to do. Run for mayor, open a florist shop, launch a singing career. Anything."

Ellen's loud sigh filled the room. "I know, and maybe that's the problem. I've got several million in the bank, earning more money than I can spend. It's mind-boggling and really difficult to wrap my mind around, even after all the publicity. I know I can do anything and I can't get my mind to settle on any one thing."

"Move to New York City and become a stripper."

Ellen's laugh was genuine. "There isn't enough silicone in the world to make this body worth looking at."

Micki's laugh joined Ellen's. "Okay, okay. Stripping's probably not for you but New York might be just the thing." Micki was still laughing as she continued. "I think you need to get away from here. It's too limiting for you."

Ellen contemplated. "I suppose I could have Dr. Okamura's office send me tapes once a week. The computer system doesn't care about where I am when I log in."

"You have all the creativity of a bowl of oatmeal. You've got all that money. Live! Quit your job. Let loose. I've been telling you for years but you just don't listen. You're too restricted here. It's time to move on. Bust out. Live for a change."

"I couldn't just quit my job. I'm the only one who can understand Dr. Okamura's accent, and I love doing it."

"Okay, okay. Keep the job if you must, but it's really time to get out of this one-horse town and find out what the real world's like."

Ellen dropped back onto the edge of her bed. "I didn't know you were so down on Fairmont. You and Milt seem to like it here and it's really not such a bad place."

"It's not bad for those of us who've found our paths. I've got Milt and the kids, PTA, scouts, lots of thing I love to do. You, however, are stagnating here and you'll never bloom. You don't date, you never do anything that's fun. You know just about every eligible man in town and you've rejected them all at one time or another. What kind of a future does that give you?"

Ellen paused, her sister's words slowly weighing her down. As always, Micki was right. Ellen had gone to school with just about everyone her age in town. She'd had a yearlong relationship with Gerry Swinburn, but that had ended when he got hired by a national brokerage firm and decided to move to New York City. "I've got to get out," he had said. "There's nothing here for me."

"What about me?" Ellen had said.

"I care for you," Gerry had answered, "but that's just not enough." He had begged her to come to New York with him, but at that time it had been out of the question. Now?

"I've got to give it a little thought," she said to her sister, "but maybe you've got a point."

After hanging up, Ellen sat on the edge of the bed in her tiny house, deep in thought. What did she have to look forward to, money or no money? What kind of future was there here for her? She worked at her computer and did little else. She was such a good customer at the local video store that they kept giving her special deals. She knew all the clerks at the local library by their first names. She owned enough romance novels to fill a wide bookshelf, and her sister teased that if she were snowed in for three years, she couldn't read them all.

What did she do all week? She saw her sister and family

several times, she went out for dinner, alone, and she went to the movies once or twice a month. She had a few friends, acquaintances actually, and she went to their houses occasionally. Sometimes she had people over. It was all routine. Predictable. Boring.

She wandered around her small, comfortable house, deep in thought. It had been her parents' house, the house she grew up in. It had two bedrooms and she still slept in the one she had shared with Micki all their growing-up years. Nothing had changed since the elder Harolds' death in a car accident four years before. Her parents' bedroom was neat and the bed made as it always had been. A rag rug covered their floor, like the one that covered hers. Ellen remembered her mother making them from scraps of faded fabric, many cut from clothes Ellen had outgrown. Hand-me-downs. She remembered the few times when she had gotten something new, something her sister hadn't already worn and could even pick out a couple of swatches.

Yet she wasn't sad about her simple upbringing. Sure her parents hadn't been wealthy, but they had been happy. The house had always smelled of something baking and there was always laughter. Her father played piano for their weekly musical evenings and, although her singing voice was abominable, she would sing along with her sister's lovely alto and her mother's lilting soprano. To make up for her lack of musical talent, she had had her watercolors, which she had used to create beautifully painted covers for the sheet music her father was always acquiring.

Ellen wandered into the living room and lifted the seat of the old piano bench. There were several of her covers still inside and she picked up one and gazed at it, a simple scene of a country meadow surrounded by apple trees. That was such a long time ago, she thought. She ran her hand over the scratched upright piano, missing the old times.

In those years, the TV was seldom on, the family preferring books and conversation to the incessant babble of the tube. When she had friends home from school they were always amazed at not being able to watch soap operas and talk shows but soon learned to enjoy the activities and the companionship of the Harold family.

Now, as Ellen wandered through the living room, the house felt lonely, empty, devoid of the joy that had always been part of her life here. Until now she hadn't even noticed how little remained, but still she was at home here, comfortable. Did she want to be just comfortable all her life? Her footsteps took her into the kitchen. Before she was born it had housed an icebox and an old kerosene stove. Now there was a ten-year-old refrigerator and a stove that was even older. But what did she cook? TV dinners, cans of ravioli, and her favorite, Kraft macaroni and cheese dinners.

She plopped herself down on a plastic-covered kitchen chair and rested her elbows on the Formica table. Where was she going in her life? She had enough money to do anything she wanted. She could redo the entire house, but it would still be a small house in a small town.

New York City. It formed the backdrop for many of the novels she enjoyed. Life pulsed there. People were busy, going from exciting place to exciting place. Fine restaurants, museums, giant bookstores, and galleries. There were so many things to do, places to see, and she certainly had the wherewithal to do it all. She didn't have to actually move there, she could stay someplace for a while and see the sights. Why not? She could put her laptop computer under her arm and visit for a month or two, find a place to stay where no one knew about her or her money. Her work would only take a few hours a day and she could explore in her free time. At least then she'd know what was out there, and if she got lonely for Micki's family, she could come back.

Over the next few days she vacillated. One minute she was hot for a trip to the big city, and the next she was terrified. How would she act? What would she do? Where would she go?

"Listen, Ellie," her sister said about three weeks after her lottery windfall, "I looked into New York City. Remember Ashley Richardson from school? Actually it's McAllister now. She was a year behind me, two ahead of you."

"Wasn't she the tall redhead with the braces? She used to come home with you at least once a week." Ellen thought. "She had a great singing voice as I remember."

"Right. Well she moved to New York City, met a guy, and got married a few years ago. We've kept in touch, so I called and asked her to do some discrete investigation. She found a small residence hotel in midtown. The east fifties, I think. It's a converted brownstone with only six apartments, not luxurious, just clean and comfortable. The building's totally secure and in a great neighborhood."

"You went behind my back?"

"Not at all. I just asked so you'd have your options open."

"Micki! How could you!" she snapped.

"Don't bite my head off because you're afraid to take the big step. If I left it up to you you'd be here until hell froze over. I'm just asking you to consider getting away, maybe for just a few weeks. We both know it would be so good for you."

"But . . ."

"I'm your sister. I've always been more of a small-town girl than you have. You've always been more of a dreamer, an adventurer."

"Me? An adventurer? Are you sure you haven't forgotten me already?"

"Not at all. You've always sold yourself short, but before,

since there wasn't anything you could do about it, I shut up. Anyway, it's really none of my business. But . . ."

Ellen raked her fingers through her hair. Some things never change. "You always say it's none of your business, then follow it up with a but."

Ellen could hear her sister's chuckle. "Right," Micki said. "You know me so well. But I know you too, Ellie. You need this. You can do this. Get a pencil and let me give you the information Ash gave me."

If only to shut Micki up, Ellen got a pencil and paper and took down the details about the hotel. "It's something between a hotel and a condo. They cater mostly to high-end one- and two-month vacationers and they supply kitchen stuff, sheets, towels, and a maid once a week. They are pretty booked, but you can call and find out when they will have a room. Ash says that it's really moderately priced for the city." Micki mentioned a monthly rent that would have choked her before the lottery winnings. "When she called, the woman said she thought they would have something for you within a month or so."

Ellen sighed, something she'd been doing a lot lately. "Maybe you're right. I'll think about it."

Later that afternoon she opened her mailbox and could barely get her mail out. She stopped at her garbage can and flipped a huge handful of solicitations. Save the Whales, MADD, cancer, kidneys, muscular dystrophy. "They never stop," she muttered.

"Hi, Ellen," her next-door neighbor said. "Nice to see you this afternoon."

Ellen looked up and saw Mrs. Cumberland bustling toward her. She had the feeling that the older woman had been watching for her. "I'm fine, Mrs. Cumberland. How are you this lovely day?"

"Really hot. This summer had been brutal so far, and my

air conditioner is on the fritz again. I just hate to have it repaired, what with saving for my grandson's college. It's so expensive."

Oh, Lord, here we go again. "I understand," Ellen said, "but do you think college is really right for Randy? He seems happy at Ernie's."

"He only thinks he's happy."

Ellen shrugged. It might be easier to just write the woman a check for ten thousand dollars, but there would always be someone else wanting more. "I've got to go in. I'll see you soon."

"Of course, dear." Ellen was sure she heard the woman murmur, "Thanks for nothing."

That was it. She'd do it. She'd spend some time in New York City where no one knew her. She'd call that hotel right away and see when they could have an apartment for her. She'd really give it all a chance. She'd stay a month, maybe more and, if she wanted to come home, she always could. This wasn't an irrevocable step, just a temporary way to see a bit of the world.

She walked from her train into the main rotunda of Grand Central Station. Actually it was what she thought Grand Central Station would look like, with marble walls and a mosaic of signs of the zodiac on the ceiling as she had seen in an article about the restoration of the old landmark. She stood in the center with streams of people flowing around her. A man bumped into her causing her to drop her pocketbook. He was tall, well-muscled, dressed in a three-piece suit fitted to his nicely proportioned body.

His hair was dark, with a small mustache and a closely trimmed beard. Wings of silver hair accented his handsome face. "I'm so sorry I jostled you," he said.

"Oh, no problem."

"Ah, but there is." He bent over to help her pick up her purse and its scattered contents. "You look a bit lost."

"Just a little."

He straightened and handed her her purse. "Are you new to the city?"

"This is my first time here."

"Well, let me help you. My limo is outside and I can take you wherever you want to go."

"I couldn't let you do that," she said.

"Of course you could. My name's Paul Broderick." He extended his hand.

"And mine's Ellen. Ellen Harold." As he took her hand she felt a jolt of electricity. God, she thought, he's a sexy man. She allowed him to lead her through the great doors and, as he had said, a stretch limousine waited at the curb. He handed her in while the chauffeur placed her suitcase in the trunk.

The interior of the limo was comfortably cool and smelled of leather and Paul's aftershave. She gave him the address of her apartment and, as they drove, he told her about himself, holding her hand throughout the journey. It was a long drive and, as they talked, he rummaged in a small cabinet and retrieved a bottle of Dom Perignon. As she sipped from a tall, slender champagne flute he stroked the back of her neck and it seemed only natural for him to take the glass from her, set it down, and touch his lips to hers.

The kiss was deep and long, their tongues gently seeking each other's deepest pleasures. His lips still in contact with hers, he pressed a button and an opaque partition slowly closed, separating them from the driver. Now they were cocooned in a world all their own.

"Paul, this is too fast," she whispered.

"Not if people know as quickly as we did how much we mean to each other." He held her shoulders. "Please. It's so right."

"Yes," she sighed, "it is."

Soon they were naked, and he stretched her out on the smooth, soft leather seat. He stroked her skin, swirling his fingers over her breasts, nuzzling her neck, his naked body against hers. "You know I won't be able to let you go," he purred in her ear. "We'll have to make our relationship more official."

"I know." Then she felt his manhood pressing against her flesh. Magically he was inside, stretching and completing her. The movements of his body gave her wonderful pleasures until he finally arched his back then collapsed.

In her bed, Ellen fell asleep.

"Oh, lord," Lucy said, sliding her palms down the thighs of her tight black leather pants. "She has the dullest, most uncreative fantasies I've ever participated in. They sound just like those romance novels she's always reading."

"Well then," Angela replied, rubbing the back of her neck beneath her flowing blond hair, "stay out of them."

"I would love to, but I checked back and her dreams have always been like scenes from bad novels. I figured that once she won the lottery she would begin having fantasies worthy of a thirty-two-year-old woman. These are puerile, suitable for a fourteen-year-old." Her fathomless black eyes flashed.

"So why don't you just let her alone? What's she to you anyway?"

"You know I'm always interested in lottery winners. I get some of my best recruits there. And you know her numbers?

They add up to 66. That's close enough to our number, mine and the boss's." She aimed her thumb downward and jabbed at her desk.

"Leave the poor woman alone, Lucy."

"But shit, Angie, she has to get a life."

"She will, and please don't call me Angie."

"Angie, Angela, Angel, what difference does it make."

"I prefer the name I selected. Angela. It's not quite so obvious."

"In order not to be obvious," Lucy snapped, tapping her long, perfect nails on the desktop, "you'd have to remove the wings."

"I wouldn't talk, lady. What about that tail of yours?"

Suddenly identical messages, in huge letters, flashed across their matching computer screens. LADIES. CEASE!

Each woman, looking chastened, tapped in a quick, YES, SIR, although the sir each referred to resided in totally different areas of the firmament.

"Well," Angela said, "anything we choose to do about Ellen will just have to wait until her future is a bit clearer."

"I guess. I just wish she'd . . ."

"Wish all you want, but let's get back to work." Each woman picked up a long printed list and began pounding on her computer keyboard. "#123,492,478, hell, #123,498,293 heaven, #123,498,012 heaven, #124,493,121 hell."

"Hold it," Angela said. "Number 121 goes to heaven."

"Not if I have anything to do with it."

"We'll just see about that."

CHAPTER 2

It took almost three weeks before the arrangements were complete. Micki had agreed to come over once a week and water her sister's plants and do whatever else needed to be done in the tiny house. She'd park Ellen's eight-year-old Toyota in her driveway and move it occasionally to keep it going, and sort the mail and send along anything important. The doctors in the medical group would send their tapes to Ellen's address in the city once a week and Ellen would update all the appropriate computer records. Since her new apartment was already furnished, she had to bring very little so she put just a few things into a box and shipped them to her new address. Ellen was delighted that the hotel was content to go month to month, so she hadn't had to sign any kind of a lease. That way she could play things by ear and move back to Fairmont whenever she pleased.

On a hot, late-August morning, Micki drove her sister to the train station in Schenectady. As the train prepared to leave, the two women hugged and shed a few final tears. "Please tell the kids I love them and I'll miss them. I'm afraid they'll forget me."

"Of course they won't. You're not going to Siberia. You'll come back and visit or move back whenever the fancy strikes you."

"I'll miss you and Milt so very much."

"I know that, he knows that, and the girls know that." Micki playfully swatted her sister on the behind. "Now get on that train and get the hell out of here."

"I love you, sis."

"I love you too, babe." Micki gave her sister a gentle shove and pushed her toward a passenger car. "Move. Now!"

Her eyes still swimming, Ellen grinned. "Yes, ma'am. I'll call you tonight." She dragged her suitcase through the train-car door just as the loud bell reminded passengers that the train was leaving. She slid into a seat and scooted over to the window, dragging her suitcase with her. As the train began to move, her eyes locked on her sister's and the two women waved. "I'm going to love being in the city," she told herself aloud. "I am doing the right thing." She wiped her tearstained cheek with the back of her hand. "And if I hate it I can always come back."

When the train was fully underway, Ellen stood and adjusted her lightweight jeans and Mickey Mouse T-shirt. Since the car wasn't crowded, she settled her suitcase more permanently on the seat beside her and gazed out the window as New York State passed beside the tracks.

She changed trains in Albany so it was late afternoon when the train crossed a river and she was suddenly surrounded by tenements spray-painted with graffiti. The train slowed and stopped at 125th Street, then plunged underground.

"Grand Central, last and final stop," the conductor's voice

boomed over the loudspeaker. "Please check around you for your personal belongings." Surrounded by bored travelers, Ellen settled her pocketbook on her shoulder, grabbed her suitcase and, as the doors opened, stepped onto a dingy platform, following the crowd into the main area of Grand Central Station. Like a tourist, which, of course, she was, she stopped in the middle of the huge main hall and looked around.

It looked exactly as she had imagined it, huge and cavernous, filled with tens of thousands of people. Since it was rush hour, hurrying commuters streamed on either side of her, hustling toward openings in the sides of the rotunda. For several minutes she just stood, staring. Most of the commuters looked hot and wrinkled in suits with jackets slung over their arms, dresses that looked limp and damp. Many of the women wore sneakers and socks and carried fancy leather attaché cases. A good percentage of the people were talking on cell phones while they walked, often skipping to one side suddenly to avoid more of the onrushing horde.

Shaking her head, and with no idea where she was going, Ellen walked toward an exit, dragging her wheeled suitcase behind her. Suddenly a man who looked remarkably like the man in her fantasy plowed headlong into her. He brushed off his three-piece suit and snapped, "Hey, watch it, lady. Don't just stand there and gawk."

"Excuse me," Ellen said, wobbling a bit before regaining her footing. Okay, so much for fantasies. Now needing air, she picked up her pace and aimed for a wide doorway to the outside. Avoiding two more collisions, she finally gained the street and, pulling her suitcase, she walked to a corner. One sign said Forty-second Street the other said Vanderbilt Avenue.

Her contact at the hotel had suggested that she take a taxi to the building but Ellen had thought that was really extravagant. Now, however, not sure of which way to walk, and totally flustered by the crowds of people, she spotted a taxi discharging a passenger right in front of her so, as a business-suited man got out, she got in. The interior of the cab smelled strongly of pine deodorant but it was cool and much quieter than the outside.

"I can put that suitcase in the trunk," the driver said with a strong Jamaican accent.

"No, thank you, I'm all right."

"Your first time in New York, Miss?" he asked as he turned down the flag on the taximeter.

"I'm from upstate," Ellen said. "It's a bit overwhelming."

"I'm sure it is at first." He sighed, looking at her in his rearview mirror. "Where to?"

When she had given him the address the driver took off with a jerk strong enough to slam her back against the seat. Fortunately Ellen was too busy staring out the windows to care about the start-stop ride. No wonder they call them the canyons of New York, she thought, gawking as she craned her neck, leaning down to try to see the tops of the buildings. She soon realized that it was impossible so she settled for looking down the side streets as the taxi moved uptown.

Finally the cab stopped in front of a beautiful building made of dark red–brown stone with a deep red door with carriage lights on either side. Ellen looked at the taximeter and almost gasped in shock. "Seventeen dollars?" she said.

"Without tip," the driver said.

"Right." She gave him a twenty-dollar bill and told him to keep the change, hoping that was enough. When he didn't offer to help her out, she opened the door and scrambled onto the sidewalk, dragging her pocketbook and suitcase behind her.

She looked up and down the side street. It was a warm evening so the street was filled with people. There was a small restaurant on the corner with a few outdoor tables, all filled now with *New Yorkers.* It amused her that she thought of Manhattanites in italics, like *them,* not us. Maybe eventually she'd feel part of it all. And if not . . .

She climbed the few steps to the front door and turned the knob. The building manager had told her about the security so she wasn't surprised that the building was locked. In Fairmont, no one locked their doors, but this was the big city so she rang the bell marked MANAGER and almost immediately an attractive woman with gray hair and deep blue eyes swung the door wide. "You must be Ellen Harold," she said, "and I've been expecting you. I'm Pam Thomas. We spoke several times on the phone. I'm here to help you with anything I can." Taking the handle of Ellen's suitcase, the woman said, "Let me show you to your apartment. You're on the second floor, number 21."

As Ellen climbed the single flight of wide, carpeted stairs, Pam prattled on about how the building had been converted into six apartments, each with a bedroom, a living room, a small eat-in kitchen, and a bath. "Everything you need can be provided, from linens to daily or weekly maid service. Just decide what you need and let me know." She took a key from her pocket and opened the door of the apartment on the right. "Home, sweet home," she said cheerily, handing Ellen two keys. "This is your apartment and this is the front door."

Pam swung the door wide and Ellen walked into a large airy room with a view of the street behind heavy security bars. The furnishings were somewhere between a motel and a regular living room: functional chairs in a navy tweed, an oatmeal sofa, and matching oatmeal drapes. The tables and small hutch were dark wood, the paintings on the wall institutional florals in muted shades of pink, blue, and beige. Ellen wondered whether the paintings had been bought to be decorative or to merely blend into the motif. Even the carpet was a tight weave of blue and beige designed, she supposed, to wear well and not show dirt. Although there were lamps and two vases filled with flowers, the room had a coldness about it.

"We just had this room completely cleaned when the previous tenant moved out so please feel free to move the furniture and add whatever little homey touches you might want." She crossed the room and opened a door. "This is the bedroom."

Ellen gazed through the door at a similarly functional room done in southwestern shades of dusty blue, soft desert pink, and beige. "And this," Pam said, pulling open a pair of beige painted louvered doors, "is your kitchen. Do you cook?"

Ellen gazed into a small room with barely enough room to change your mind. It had the requisite appliances, with a tiny table and diminutive chairs. "I do, but I imagine I'll be eating out most of the time."

Pam spent the next fifteen minutes filling Ellen in on the building regulations, the maid service, and the location of the nearest laundry, dry cleaners and such. Finally she said, "Well, I'm sure you want to get settled, so I'll leave you. I live in 11, just below you, so if you need anything, just ring my bell. Tomorrow perhaps we can sit together and get to know each other. Once you've been here a few days, I'll be glad to answer any questions about the neighborhood, where to eat, where to shop, and things like that."

"That would be wonderful. I'll just ring your bell."

For several weeks Ellen prowled Manhattan. She visited museums, enjoyed some and was bored by others. She went to seven Broadway shows, enjoyed most and was bored to tears by two. And she walked. She window-shopped along almost every street and avenue, ending up on a few occasions in less-than-desirable neighborhoods.

She ate at fancy restaurants and felt a bit embarrassed at being frequently asked, "Will someone be joining you?" She found she was much more comfortable at a tiny luncheonette around the corner from her apartment where she read while she ate or just listened to the counterman yelling, "Scramble two, whiskey down, bacon and burn it."

She received the packet of tapes each Tuesday and by Friday she had entered the information into the computer and modemed it back to the office in Fairmont.

Almost a month after moving to the city she was on the phone with her sister for their weekly chat. "I've been thinking about coming back home."

"Ellen, why? We've discussed and discussed it. There's nothing here for you right now."

"There's nothing here for me either. I tried it, and I've enjoyed parts of my visit but it's over now and I'm coming home."

"Ridiculous. You've only just tasted the tip of the New York City iceberg. Jump into the pool. Swim around. Indulge."

"In what? I'm bored. I have nothing much to do and I can't just wander around like a gypsy." Ellen propped her feet on the small wooden coffee table and crossed her ankles. *I want to go home,* she confessed to herself. *I feel like a fish out of water here. Am I slinking home like a coward? Not giving it a chance? Do I really have to give it a chance?*

"Haven't you met anyone to pal around with?"

"Not really. I've spent some time with Pam, the gal who runs this place, but she's got her own friends and she goes out every night. She's friendly enough, but it's just not my style."

"I had hoped you'd meet some men there, date, you know."

"Yeah, right. No such luck."

"Have you made any efforts to be social?"

Ellen sat up and shifted the phone to her other ear. "You mean like go to a bar and sit around waiting for some man to ask me what my sign is?"

"Not that, but, well you know."

"Actually no, I don't know. I have no idea how to meet people of either sex."

"So why don't you do something. Take a course, volunteer somewhere where there are people."

Ellen settled back. She'd indulge her sister, listen to her suggestions as she always had, then go home. She'd had enough.

"I can't do all your thinking for you but maybe it's time you did something you always wanted to do. Take an art course for instance. You were always the talented one. Remember those watercolors you did for Dad's music? Since it's getting into fall, how about volunteering for a political candidate or at a local hospital?"

Art course. That was an idea, something she hadn't thought of. "Hmm," she said after a moment. "That's not a bad idea. Actually that's two good ideas you just had."

"Which ones?" Micki asked, her voice brightening.

"I could take an art course. I've always thought I had a little talent. There's a gallery a few blocks from here and according to the sign in the window the owner runs classes on the mornings when the gallery is closed."

"You said two ideas."

Ellen's eyes brightened. She might just do that. "The hospital volunteering isn't bad either. There are so many hospitals in the city, I could maybe read to patients or volunteer in the gift shop." Giggling, she said, "You know I just caught myself. I was thinking that I couldn't do something without getting paid, you know like a real job. But hell, I don't need the money, do I? I could just do it because I want to."

Micki's warm voice narrowed the distance between Fairmont and New York City. "You sure could. I think that sounds wonderful. Go for it, girl."

Later that afternoon Ellen pulled on a pair of well-worn jeans and a faded T-shirt and, since with the beginning of fall it was getting a bit cooler, she added a light windbreaker. She walked the few blocks to a storefront with a large gold-lettered sign announcing The Templeton Gallery. In the corner of the window sat a small carefully printed card stating that art classes were available. She strolled inside and looked around. The walls were painted stark white, one scattered with landscapes, several of windblown rocky coasts, some of pastoral forest glens. Another wall was covered with still lifes of fruit baskets, flowers, china, and crystal while two other walls were hung with portraits. As she peered at the signatures she saw that each wall featured a different artist. She sighed and stared at a particularly dramatic seascape, muttering, "I wish I could paint like that."

"Do you paint?" a male voice behind her asked.

Startled, she turned and gazed into a pair of sexy deep-blue eyes. "Just a little."

"Many people have undiscovered talent, just waiting for the right situation to unleash it. Maybe you're one of those."

Ellen tore her gaze from the man's eyes and took in the whole man. He was tall, and towered over her five-foot-three-inch frame. He had coal-black hair that flopped over his forehead and a tightly cropped beard and mustache that gave his handsome face a distinguished look. She guessed that he was around her age.

"Are you?" he asked again, his words musical with a slight Irish brogue.

"Am I what?" Ellen said, dragging her mind back to the present.

"Are you a vessel of undiscovered talent?"

Ellen snorted at the absurdity of the comment. "I doubt that, but I have been thinking of taking an art class. I used to paint watercolors back when I was younger, before my parents died. My sister always said I had talent." She slammed her mouth shut when she realized that she was rambling.

"I'm sure you do and maybe a class is just the thing." He extended his right hand and Ellen noticed the heavy coat of black hair that covered his wrist, below the turned-up sleeves of his light blue shirt. "I'm Kevin Duffy and I run this gallery. I also give classes upstairs Monday, Wednesday, and Friday mornings. I have one specifically on watercolors each Wednesday although we're pretty flexible around here and the classes usually focus on techniques necessary to any artist, regardless of the medium."

Since it seemed rude not to shake his hand, Ellen took it and marveled at the warmth and strength of his grasp. He held her hand just a moment longer than was necessary, gazing into her eyes with almost hypnotic intensity. Then they separated and he strode to a desk and returned with his card and several flyers. "This is me," he said, handing her his card, "and this is the schedule of classes. There's no strict regimen so once we get you settled, you can come any time, attend one class or several. It would be entirely up to you." He pulled a pen from his pocket and ticked off the classes on Wednesdays. "As I said, this is a class in basic watercolor techniques." He looked into her eyes again. "The classes are a bit pricey, but well worth it if you're thinking about getting serious about your work. I suggest that you take a class, free of charge of course, so you can taste what we do. Then you can decide whether the cost would be justified."

Ellen could barely get her breath. "Oh, I think I can manage the cost." She took the paper. "You know, I might just try it."

Still gazing into her eyes, Kevin handed her another sheet of paper. "This is a list of some of the basic supplies. You probably have some of the items, but there's a lot of stuff you need if you really want to paint seriously. Of course, the items with the stars next to them are the only ones really necessary, the rest are just nice to have. The right paper's important, of course, and the quality of the colors."

"Oh yes, I'm sure they are."

"There's an art supply store I can recommend on Twenty-seventh Street. Ben Kellogg, the owner, really knows his stuff. If you ask for him and tell him you're a friend of mine taking a course, he can steer you toward the right equipment." Kevin took one of the sheets from her and wrote the address and the owner's name on the back.

At that moment, the phone rang and Kevin, seeming reluctant, turned to answer it. "Maybe I'll see you at the class next Wednesday."

"Oh yes," she sighed as he grabbed the phone and began a lengthy conversation. "You certainly will."

She found the art store and enlisted the assistance of the owner, who was more helpful when she casually announced that she was new to serious watercolor and needed start-up supplies. She listened to the man rattle on about Kordofan gum and oxgall and the differences between pan and tube watercolors. He regaled her with the advantages of small sable brushes and wider synthetic ones and, of course, she just had to have a short, flat boar bristle one. He spent almost half an hour discussing paper—single sheets, pads, and blocks—then helped her select charcoal and graphite drawing sticks and several thicknesses of pencils. By the time she had gathered only the "most basic" supplies she had spent more than two hundred dollars.

At home, Ellen unwrapped her purchases, opened a large sketch pad and sharpened a stick of charcoal on the sandpaper pad as she had been shown. With a few quick strokes she created the shape of a face with a short beard and piercing eyes. While it didn't really look like Kevin, it was obvious that she had him in mind. Three hours passed while she made drawing after drawing of men with beards and graceful hands.

Finally empty of ideas, she made herself a pot of macaroni and cheese and, bowl in hand, stretched out on the sofa with her feet on the coffee table. When she finished, she set the bowl down and closed her eyes.

She walked into Kevin's studio to begin her classes, but as she looked around at the garret-like room she discovered that she was alone. No other students this morning? She was sure he had said Wednesday.

Kevin emerged from a back room, dressed in a pair of khaki pants and a paint-splattered shirt, both hugging his muscular body. "I knew you'd be here."

"I c-c-came for class," Ellen whispered.

"No you didn't," Kevin said, taking her paint box from her shaking fingers. "You came for me."

Ellen gazed into his deep-blue eyes, unable to tear her gaze away.

"You came because you knew we'd be here alone, aching for each other. Tell me you knew." He held her upper arms in his steely grip. When she remained silent, he whispered again, "Tell me."

His lips were against her hair and she could feel the heat of him even through their clothes. Had she known? "Yes," she said, "I knew."

Ellen leaned against him and he enfolded her within his warmth and surrounded her with the manly scent of him. She lay her cheek against his chest, listening to the accelerated beat of his heart, deep and steady. "God, I want you," he said, the sound rumbling in his chest.

Ellen raised her hands until her palms lay splayed against his shirtfront. "And I want you."

His lips met hers in a searing kiss, one that flowed through her body like molten lava.

"Okay," Lucy said in the computer room, slamming her hand on the table, "I've had enough of her girlish romantic fantasies. They sound like every mushy novel ever written. Let's get real here. Life isn't like that. Love at first sight. I've been waiting for you." She made a rude noise. "God, it's such slop."

"Don't, Luce," Angela said, looking up from her screen. "Don't get involved in Ellen's fantasies. It's not nice."

"Nice. Pooh." She ran her blood-red nails through her long, straight, black hair. "That woman is going to fantasize herself into heartbreak. She's got that man so tangled up in her dreams that she's bound to be disappointed. She's dreaming of him like he's some kind of paragon of manhood, handsome and sexy, a man who knows all the right moves. Next she'll be thinking about how he prowls like a jungle cat. What she needs is a real man and a real fantasy. Good, hot, sweaty sex with lots of hands and mouths, cocks and pussies."

"Lucy, really. Watch your language. My boss might be listening."

"He created great sex so why shouldn't we all enjoy it. The words are just ways of accelerating the heartbeat and arousing the libido."

Angela glared, but said nothing. "Now," Lucy said, tapping a nail against her front teeth. "I'll just create a real fantasy for Ellen and see how she likes it."

Angela sighed and shook her head, knowing that once Lucy got an idea into her head she couldn't or wouldn't be talked out of it.

"Okay, where was she . . ."

Ellen stood in the warm garret with Kevin's arms around her, enjoying the beat of his heart. Suddenly he picked her up in his arms and carried her to the bed in the corner of the studio, then he began to unbutton his shirt. "What . . . ?" Ellen whispered.

"You know why you came. To be with me. Now we can do it all. Let's get naked."

Back in the computer room Angela snapped, "If you make her dream like that, you'll drive her schizo. If you want to change her fantasies, you have to be gentle and gradual. 'Let's get naked' indeed. Go easy or she'll bolt."

Lucy heaved a sigh. "Okay. I guess you're right. I just like to get right to the good stuff."

"Just a little push. Okay?"

"Right. Just a little push in the right direction."

"You know why you came to me. Let me love you the way you were meant to be loved."

"I want that, but I'm afraid."

"I would never hurt you," Kevin said. Then he cupped her face in his hands and brushed his mouth across hers. "I would never do anything you didn't want."

She let out a long breath. "I know," she purred, moving her face to taste his lips. She slid her hands up his chest and held his broad shoulders. "Yes, I know."

Then his hands stroked down her ribs and slipped beneath her sweater to caress her bare skin. Heat. Her skin burned with molten fire everywhere he touched. Lava flowed through her body, to her breasts, between her legs. She could barely breathe, barely think. She wanted to remember every moment of their time together but her mind was in a whirl trying to cope with the sensations bombarding her. His mouth opened and hers opened beneath it. Their tongues dueled, their bodies blending, pressing against each other.

His palms stroked heated paths up her sides to her back where he deftly unhooked her bra. His fingers traced an erotic path to her aching breasts. He plucked at her erect nipples, drawing feelings from her that she hadn't known she possessed. Quaking with need Ellen grabbed the back of Kevin's shirt and pulled it from his pants so she could slide beneath and touch his skin. Her hands wouldn't be still, touching, scratching, urging him on. She tangled her fingers in the heavy hair on his chest, finding and caressing his small nipples.

With a single motion, he pulled her sweater over her head, then dragged her bra off and tossed it in a corner. His eyes devoured her naked skin while he tugged off his shirt and pants. When he stood, naked, in the middle of the small room his arousal was obvious.

Ellen just stared. His nude body was gorgeous with wide shoulders and narrow hips. Her eyes devoured him, avoiding only the nest of dark hair that filled his groin. "Yes, look at me," he purred. "Look your fill, but I want to look at you, too."

He quickly unbuckled her belt and dragged her jeans off until she stood wearing only tiny white lace panties. "So beautiful," he said, his eyes telling her how gorgeous he thought she looked. He closed the small dis-

tance between them and held her close so that the entire length of him pressed against the entire length of her. She could feel his hardness against her belly.

"Okay," Lucy said, "it's time for them to get it on."

With one motion he grabbed the front of her panties and ripped them from her body. He cupped her buttocks and lifted her, fitting his mouth over hers, pulling her legs around his waist. The tip of his cock pressed against her opening and with one violent thrust he was inside of her. Still standing in the center of the room, his strong arms held her, raising and lowering her body so his cock slid deep inside, then withdrew. Over and over he fucked her until she was mad with it, holding his strong shoulders, grasping his hips with her legs.

With a roar of triumph, he lifted her so he could bite her erect nipple and, with the shard of pleasure/pain, she felt her body convulse around his cock. He lowered her to the floor, never leaving his place inside her, then pounded into her, driving his cock still deeper until, with a bellow, he came.

"Phew," Angela said. "You do create a great love scene, Luce."

"Love, shmove. It's good hot sex that counts." Lucy settled behind her desk. "You know, I think she's a candidate for Margaret Mary. It's about time Ellen learned about life and men and great sex, and Margaret Mary's just the woman who can do it."

"I have to agree but you know that she hates it when you call her Margaret Mary. It's Maggie and she's perfect for this job."

*   *   *

In her living room Ellen awoke with a start. She remembered the dream in vivid detail and her hands shook with the memories. She had never before had such an erotic one, so detailed. It was as if she could still feel the man's . . . the man's . . . well feel the man inside of her. She touched the crotch of her jeans and found herself hot and damp. "Phew," she said. "That was some dream. I wonder where it came from."

"Probably from your subconscious," a woman's soft voice said.

Ellen jumped so suddenly that she almost fell off the sofa. She whirled around and saw a woman standing at the window, gazing out onto Fifty-second Street. She looked about fifty, with curly black hair and deep brown eyes. "I used to live around here, you know," she said. "It's such a great neighborhood."

"H-H-How did you get in here? Who the hell are you? Get out of my apartment!" Ellen was almost shrieking. Was she losing her mind?

"Actually I can't. I've been sent here to do a job and I really have to do it. It might mean the difference between Heaven and Hell for me."

"Out! Now! I don't care who you are or what you're here for. Out!" Ellen couldn't keep her voice from quaking, afraid she would burst into tears if the woman didn't leave.

"Relax and I'll explain. You're Ellen Harold and I'm Maggie Sullivan. I'm here to help you and once you understand all that we have to do, we'll get along just fine." She sighed. "It's always hardest at the beginning but you will get used to it. I promise." She twisted a strand of hair around her index finger. "Sit down and give me a few minutes to explain. Okay?"

Ellen made a supreme effort and controlled her voice. Sounding much calmer than she felt, she said, "No. I'm sorry but no. Whatever you're selling I don't want any. Whatever you're advocating, I'm against it. Just leave and we'll forget this little incident ever happened."

"I told you, I can't leave. I'm afraid I'm here to stay." She bustled to the tiny kitchen area and opened the miniature refrigerator. "Have you got any wine around here? I think we could both use a glass."

CHAPTER 3

Numbly, Ellen pointed to the cabinet over the sink. "There's a bottle of cabernet in there and the glasses are in the same cabinet." Why couldn't she get this person to leave? She stared at the woman called Maggie and tried to decide who or what she was. Dressed in a calf-length flowered-print skirt and a soft gauzy rose-colored blouse, she had warm, toast-brown eyes and an open face that at any other time Ellen would have trusted. Nevertheless, Ellen decided that in one more minute she'd have to call the cops and get this loony out of her apartment.

Maggie unscrewed the top from the wine bottle, half-filled two glasses and offered one to Ellen. "Don't call the cops just yet," she said. "Give me a few moments and I promise you'll understand. Really."

Ellen accepted the wine and took a swallow of the harsh red liquid. Maggie sipped and coughed. "Blah," she said. "You'd think that with all your money you wouldn't have to drink this sheep dip. I'll drink almost anything but this is almost too awful for me."

"Sheep dip?" Ellen said softly. "It's good red wine, and what the hell do you know about my money. Is this some kind of kidnapping? You want ransom?"

Ignoring Ellen's questions, Maggie said, "This is true sheep dip. It's overly tannic, lacks any real fruit and has a finish that tastes like furniture polish. And no, this isn't a kidnapping and there's no ransom."

Ellen just shook her head. The wine tasted like all the red wines she'd ever had. Even if it were bad she wouldn't let this woman have the satisfaction of showing it. "I think it's just fine." She took another large gulp.

"Okay. Lessons on wine. That's on the list."

"What list?"

"Let me start at the beginning so you'll understand—well at least as much as I understand. But first, what's today's date?"

"Date?"

"Today's date. What is it?"

"It's September 28."

"What year?"

With no clue as to what was going on, Ellen answered, "1999."

"I've been dead for more than four years."

"Right, and I'm the tooth fairy. You know," Ellen said, "maybe you should sit down. Is there some relative I can call to come and pick you up?" *Where has this loony escaped from and how can I get her to voluntarily go back there? Soon. Now.*

"I'm dead. I don't know any other way of explaining it to you. Your reaction is really predictable and I can certainly understand your reluctance to accept me. Actually I've met several women in the last few years and each one of them has reacted the same way." She gazed into space. "I've got to think of a better way to break the news about myself. I'll have to think about that. Maybe in the future I should just say that I'm a fairy godmother." She returned her gaze to Ellen. "Any way you slice it, however, I'm a ghost, sent here to help you with your life."

"I don't need any help with my life, and I don't care whether you think you're Napoleon or Moses. It's time for you to leave." Ellen rose from the sofa and started toward the apartment door.

Maggie shrugged. "I told you I can't leave and, for the moment, neither can you, but you can give it a try. It might help clarify a few things." She motioned toward the door so Ellen crossed the room and turned the knob. Nothing happened. The knob turned beneath her hand as it was supposed to, but the latch didn't move. She pulled at the door but it wouldn't open. "Open this door!" she shouted.

"I can't. It's not under my control. We're stuck here until we understand each other."

"Okay. I'm calling the cops."

"That won't work either, but you're welcome to try. Go for it."

Ellen picked up the phone and heard the familiar dial tone, yet when she pushed the buttons, nothing happened. The dial tone continued as though she hadn't dialed at all. "Who set this all up? Are you here to rob me? You obviously know about the money so how much do you want?"

"I told you, I don't want money. I only want to help you."

Since the apartment was only on the second floor and overlooked a busy street she could shout for help. Ellen tried the window but, like the door, it wouldn't open. Maggie gracefully settled on the far end of the long sofa, spread her skirt around her, and sipped her wine, making an ugly face as she did so. "Now, can we talk?"

Ellen looked from the door to the window to the phone, then dropped onto the far end of the couch with her hand on the telephone. As soon as this was all ironed out she was calling the cops and that was that. "Okay, talk but just make it quick. And please, no 'I'm dead' stuff. I'm not that crazy yet."

"I am dead and there's no help for that. I died in 1995 of a sudden heart attack."

Just humor her, then she'll go away. "Okay, you're dead. I believe you." *Just let her talk until she's ready to get the hell out of here.*

"I can prove that part if you'll just come with me into the bathroom." When Maggie stood and walked toward the small bath Ellen reluctantly followed. Maggie directed her to stand in front of the mirror and Maggie positioned herself behind her. Ellen gazed into the mirror and saw her reflection clearly, but in the mirror she was alone. She turned and, sure enough, the woman stood just behind her shoulder, but, as Ellen's gaze returned to the mirror she was by herself. No Maggie, no wineglass, no nothing.

"I don't reflect," Maggie said, "because I'm dead. Only you can see or hear me."

Ellen stared, then turned several times to assure herself that the woman was right. Maggie didn't reflect. What the hell was going on? Ellen rubbed her forehead, now totally confused.

Together the two women walked back into the living room. "Okay. Let's say I believe that," Ellen said. *Although I don't.*

"I know you don't but you will, eventually. Let me try to explain a bit more. Before I died, I was a very high-priced

call girl—or I guess you'd say a call woman in my case."
They settled onto opposite ends of the sofa.

"A hooker?" *Sure, right. Fine. That tops it all. A dead
prostitute. Right.*

"You know, I've learned to hate the word *hooker*. I was
a wonderful woman who just happened to have sex for
money. Some women will put out for dinner and a movie, I
just took the cash."

"Well, that's a unique attitude," Ellen said her voice heavy
with sarcasm.

"It's not unique at all. I merely entertained lonely men.
We went to dinner, had great conversations, shared lots of
laughs and ended up in bed together—actually in bed and
other places. They gave me money because they enjoyed
what we did together and wanted to reward me, compensate
me for my time. It was just that simple."

Ellen looked a bit less incredulous as she said, "You make
it sound like a lark. What about love and marriage?"

"Love is wonderful, don't get me wrong." Maggie un-
crossed and recrossed her legs spreading her skirt artfully
around her. "I have loved several men in my time but good
hot sex has little to do with love with a capital *L*. It's loving
of a different sort. I cared about my clients. I wanted to make
them happy and they wanted the same for me. We cared
about one another. That didn't mean, however, that we
wanted to spend our lives together, walking hand in hand
down the yellow brick road. A great roll in the hay on occasion was enough."

What the woman was saying seemed to make sense, somehow, at least for her. "Okay, okay. You don't need to get
up on your soapbox. Whatever you did, you did, but that
still doesn't answer the basic question. What the heck are
you doing here? I certainly have no intention of becoming a

hooker—sorry, call woman—so what's this all about?" Ellen listened to what she had just said. Had she really accepted that she was talking to the ghost of a dead prostitute?

"You're my latest case. Lucy and Angela sent me to try to wake you up to the possibilities in your life."

"I don't need any help, thank you. I'm doing just fine."

"If you're so fine, then why did you just have that long conversation with your sister?"

"How the hell . . . ?" Ellen saw the small smile on Maggie's face. "Okay, but I'm fine. Tell your friends to butt out!"

"Lucy and Angela don't butt out easily. They send me on assignment and I'm stuck until they decide I've done my job. If I don't complete my mission I have no idea what happens. Maybe I end up in Hell after all."

"End up in Hell?" Ellen tucked her legs beneath her and held her wineglass in front of her, almost as protection against what she was going to hear. "Okay, explain. I'm listening."

"Where to begin? More than four years ago, I had a fatal heart attack, after which I just appeared in the computer room." As Ellen started to interrupt, Maggie held up her hand. "Let me tell this in my own way. It's difficult enough to believe any way you slice it, but it's all true." Ellen's body relaxed.

"The computer room is the place where the 'up or down' decisions are made about everyone who dies. You understand, Heaven or Hell. Most cases are easy, I gather. Either Angela, she's an angel you understand, or Lucy, she's a representative of Lucifer, gets the poor slob and it's off to transportation. Then what? I've no idea.

"Anyway, they had a problem with me. I was a prostitute so by rights should have gone . . ." Maggie made a thumbs-down gesture. "However, I was a really good person, helping people sexually and other ways. I was kind to children and animals, well you get the idea. So Angela argued on my behalf as I sat there about as confused as you are now. Finally the two women decided on a test for me. They sent me down to earth to help a woman named Barbara to learn about her sexuality. Barbara blossomed, with my help of course, but in the end that didn't really make the decision for them. So Lucy and Angela decided to keep me on for a while as a consultant. They send me to earth from time to time to help someone." Maggie took a swallow of wine, and grimaced. "We really have to improve your taste in wine." She set the glass on the coffee table. "You are my latest assignment."

"Why me? What did I do to warrant this attention? Whatever it was, I want to undo it."

"Actually Lucy frequently plays the lottery, or plays with it, and she's particularly interested in winning numbers that add up to 66 like yours did."

"I'll bite. Why 66?"

"Second cousin to 666, the devil's number. When you won, she brought you up on her computer and thought you and I would get along well."

"She thought that I needed someone to tinker with my life? You can tell her that my life is just fine, thank you." Ellen cupped her hands around her mouth and faced the ceiling. "Listen, Lucy, Angela, take your minion and go," she called loudly. "Vamoose, scram. Find someone else to play with. I'm just fine."

"You're really not as fine as you could be. Your sex life is a mess and that's what I'm here to correct. Lucy told me about your fantasies."

Ellen bolted from the sofa. "They know my fantasies?"

"They know just about everything, and Lucy isn't a great fan of your dreams. She tweaked your last one, you know."

Ellen remembered the dream she was having right before

Maggie's appearance. It had been different from her usual. Vastly different. Shit. "Shit!" She swallowed hard. "Sorry."

"Don't be. I've heard all those words before and sometimes they can add spice to your language."

"Assuming I believe all this, which I'm still not sure I do, I don't want you. I like my sex life the way it is. Just go away."

"You may not want me, but you need me, and I need you. I have a job to do and you're it."

"Okay, so what exactly is your job? What do I have to do to get you to go away?"

"It's really what *we* have to do. We have to help you understand about sex."

"I already understand about sex; my mother educated me just fine. I know about intercourse, condoms, the whole nine yards. What else is there?"

"Oh, my darling," Maggie said, "there's so much. As the Carpenters said, 'We've only just begun.' "

Ellen sighed. "I will admit that right now my sex life is a bit on the thin side, but that's bound to change in the near future."

"Thin?" Maggie stood and began to prowl the room. "Your sex life is non-existent and if you continue the way you're going it won't improve anytime during this millennium or the next. You're stuck in a sexless rut. You have a tiny opinion of yourself so you're defeated before you start. Your fantasies are unrealistic and you're constantly disappointed that the real world isn't like the one you imagine."

"Thanks," Ellen said dryly.

"It's the truth. You sit here with all the resources of the city spread in front of you, and enough money to enjoy them to the fullest." She stopped and focused on Ellen. "Look at this room. It looks like no one lives here. No plants, no pictures, no old magazines. No old anything. It's all sterile, as if you're just waiting to run back to your small town."

"I really don't want your opinion."

"I don't care what you want. I'm going to tell you a few things you need to hear. You're like a butterfly, too afraid of the outside world to come out. You peek out of your cocoon with a little periscope and you never *experience* anything."

"Oh, please. Really."

"That's you. Miss Sexual Underachiever of the Month— of the Decade. Now, however, you have the opportunity to change all that with me to help you every step of the way." She sat back down on the sofa and took Ellen's hand. "Be honest with yourself just this once. Wouldn't you like to be a bit more interesting to men? Wouldn't you like to have a few dates, go out for dinner occasionally, climb into bed with a horny guy and let him make you seriously crazy for an entire night? Doesn't that thought curl your toes?"

As Ellen started to give the standard answer, she looked into Maggie's eyes. If she were to be completely honest, what Maggie was suggesting sounded really good. She wanted to be attractive to men. She wanted a man to look at her the way Kevin had but not, as she accepted, because she was a potential client with an open wallet. She wanted a real sex life.

When she didn't respond, Maggie continued, "I thought so. I'm grateful that, at least inside your head, you're being honest." She reached over and held Ellen's hand tightly. "Let me do what I know how to do. It won't hurt and I won't make you do anything you don't want to do. I can help, really I can, with your looks, your clothes, but most of all with your attitude. Please."

Ellen sighed. She realized that she had accepted everything

this woman said. Maggie was the spirit of a dead prostitute who had been sent to help her become a sex goddess.

"Not a sex goddess, just a woman who knows her own worth, in and out of bed."

Ellen expelled a long breath, then lifted her glass. "I guess I have nothing to lose."

Maggie picked up her wineglass and the two women touched rims. "To the future, and how we can improve it together." They sipped and Maggie made a face. "And here's to better wine."

Ellen sipped. "Better wine? Isn't this the way wine is supposed to taste?"

"Not on your life. Let me give you a demonstration of what we can achieve together."

Ellen's eyes brightened. This could be really good. "Are you going to zap up a bottle of something terrific?"

"I don't zap anything. Actually I've been after Lucy and Angela to give me the power, you know, like Michael Landon in *Highway to Heaven,* but so far, nothing." She looked at Ellen seriously. "What I meant was let's go to the wine store and buy something special. Then we can have a taste comparison and you'll see what you've been missing. Let's make that a symbol of what you've been missing in the rest of your life. It's getting late but in this neighborhood there's always an open liquor store."

With a great sigh, Ellen decided to go along with Maggie, at least for the moment. As they left the apartment, Ellen noticed that the door opened without any problem. She guessed that Lucy and Angela were satisfied that she wouldn't run away and spoil Maggie's plans.

A few minutes later the two women were inside a small neighborhood store. "Let's get something a bit pricey for our first try. Later I can teach you how to get a nice wine for under twenty dollars a bottle." Maggie puttered around the racks on the wall. "For now, however," she said, returning to Ellen's side, "let's splurge."

"Okay. What should I get?"

"Are you talking to me?" A small man with a potbelly strode over, his balding head sweating slightly. Puffing, he said, "Can I help you with something?"

"I'd like a bottle of nice red wine," Ellen said. She turned to Maggie. "Did you see anything you liked?"

"I like everything we stock," the man said.

"Remember that he can't see me so he has no idea you're not talking to him," Maggie said. "Just let him suggest and I'll steer you to something sensational." She paused. "Tell him you need a really nice bottle of red wine for a really fancy dinner you're attending. Maybe a cabernet sauvignon."

Ellen repeated Maggie's words, stumbling slightly over the word *sauvignon*.

"Of course," the clerk said, obviously dubious about her knowledge of wine. "How about this?" He led her to a rack on one wall. "We have some nice Australian cabs, not quite as expensive as the really fine Californias. These are nice wines with good fruit and well within the average pocketbook."

"Nope," Maggie said. "Tell him you want a good California cab."

"Cab?" Ellen whispered.

"Short for cabernet," Maggie explained.

"Excuse me?" the clerk said, totally confused by Ellen's apparent talking to herself.

"I'd like a good California cab."

"Of course." He bustled to another area of the store and pulled out another bottle. "How about this?"

Maggie leaned over and read the label. "Not bad. Ask him whether he has a 1990. That was a superb year. It might be a bit over the hill, but I loved the nineties."

"Do you have a 1990? That was a superb year."

The clerk's body straightened. "Nothing quite that old, I'm afraid but some of the more recent vintages are just wonderful. I might have something you'd enjoy over here." He walked to a corner and touched a rack of bottles reverently. "These aren't cheap, but you should like them if you're looking for a really good cab. I can, of course, take you into the cellar in the back for the really fine wines."

Maggie gazed at the rack and grinned. She pointed to one bottle, a Mount Eden Estate Bottled cabernet. "Take that one."

Ellen looked at the price. "Fifty-five dollars?" she gasped.

"I told you it would be a bit high-priced," the clerk said. "I can certainly find something else. You can have the regular estate bottled, rather than the Old Vine Reserve. It's only thirty-five."

"Take the Old Vine," Maggie said.

Ellen looked doubtful but Maggie vehemently nodded. With a shrug Ellen pointed to the more expensive bottle and said, "Okay. I'll take this one."

A bit bemused at the double conversations, the clerk lifted the bottle and took it to the cash register. "Cash or credit?"

Ellen pulled out her credit card and handed it to the clerk. "You know," Ellen said to Maggie, "I'm not sure I have a corkscrew."

"I beg your pardon?" the clerk said.

Maggie pointed to a hanging display. "That one will do fine." Ellen pulled a deep red contraption off the rack and dropped it on the counter.

As the man turned to his credit-card reader, Ellen could hear him mutter, "She buys a fifty-five dollar bottle of wine and doesn't even have a corkscrew." She watched his head shake as the machine printed her receipt. It was all Ellen could do not to giggle.

Back in the apartment, Maggie withdrew the bottle from the brown paper bag and put it on the coffee table. With new glasses from the kitchen, she showed Ellen how to use the corkscrew and how to properly pour the wine. "At least you have the right glasses," Maggie said, holding the wine-filled glass up to the light.

"All this is such silliness: right glass, right year. Wine makers put the mystery in it so folks like me will spend a lot of money on the stuff, afraid to do something wrong."

"Not really. The shape of the glass is important for holding the nose properly. You grasp it by the stem so you don't change the temperature or get finger marks on the outside of the glass. A clean, clear glass helps you see the wine and enjoy the color." Maggie held the wine up to the light. "Look at that gorgeous baby."

Ellen looked. "Nice," she said, unimpressed.

"Okay. We'll get to color later. Do this." Maggie swirled the wine around the glass and Ellen did the same. "Now stick your nose in there and inhale."

"Wow," Ellen said as she breathed in. "It smells really nice."

Maggie smiled. "You only half fill the glass so you can swirl it and let the shape of the glass capture the aroma, the nose. I'm not going to bore you with a lesson on bouquet right now, I just want you to know there's more to wine than just the taste. Now take a small amount in your mouth, and try to gently inhale at the same time. Taste is mostly smell." She watched as Ellen tried to inhale and sip at the same time.

"Holy cow," Ellen said, relishing the exploding flavors in her mouth. "That's wonderful. I love it."

"I knew you would." She handed Ellen her glass from earlier. "Taste this now."

Ellen sipped the screw-cap wine that she and Maggie had been drinking and scrunched her face. "This really shouldn't be called the same stuff." She put that glass down and picked up the glass of the California cab, taking another sip. "I have to admit it. You were right."

"I'm right about a lot of things. Sex is the same as wine. The more you learn and the more you experience, the better it gets."

"I'm starting to believe you." Ellen sipped the wine, smiling as the tastes and smells bombarded her senses. "Maybe you do have something to teach me."

Maggie grinned. "I certainly do, and I'm beginning to think that I've got something pretty nice to work with." She touched the lip of her glass to Ellen's. "To new frontiers in wine and everything else."

For the first time Ellen felt excited about her future. "This might just be fun."

"It will be a blast."

"Where do we start?"

Maggie reached into the side pocket of her skirt. "I have— sorry, had—a good friend named CJ. He writes great erotic stories and records them on CDs." She withdrew a slender CD jewel case. "You need to understand what good sex is about, to expose yourself to new and exciting realities. I know that you've got a CD player so just relax and listen to the first one of these. Open your mind and pretend the woman is you."

Ellen took the CD and looked at it, puzzled. *Just After Midnight—A Collection of Erotic Stories by CJ Winterman. Read by the author.* "Erotic stories? Me? Why?"

"I think I told you about Barbara. She was the first woman I helped and I gave her some stories on CD too. She found that they really gave her a new look at sex. She learned that whatever people do that doesn't hurt anyone is okay. From your fantasies, I gather you've had very little experience."

"I wouldn't say that?" Ellen said, thinking that she actually would say that.

"Let's just say that I'd like to broaden your mental horizons before I try to broaden your physical ones. These stories are all about the power of magic to give us the freedom to do and say what we want. Listen to one or two a night, and see how you feel. I suggested that Barbara listen in the bathtub with a glass of wine, all nice and relaxed. You might find that some of the things the people do curl your toes, some things might not be your taste. Just understand what's out there so you learn what you want and what you don't. Then we'll take steps to try and get it for you."

"Why the title *Just After Midnight*?"

"At midnight people become a little bit more adventurous. The characters in the stories use magic to create adventure but in real life we sometimes need to push ourselves out of the nest and be daring, creating our own magic. With the right outlook it can be midnight at any time of the day."

"Okay. I'll listen to a story if you want me to." Ellen was surprised that in the space of a few hours she'd accepted Maggie and decided to take her advice. This was almost as much of an upheaval as winning the lottery. "I won't promise anything."

"Of course you won't and I don't expect you to. The stories are also great for communication. One woman I worked with played them for her boyfriend. They listened together and he was just as turned on as she was. They learned a lot about each other and their desires, too."

"I guess two people could exchange ideas that way without having to talk."

"You got it." She patted the hand that held the CD. "It's

getting late and I've got to be going now. I don't know when I'll be back, it just sort of happens. The next time I see you, we'll have lots to do."

"There's one thing I need for you to do when you see those friends of yours. Tell them to butt out of my fantasies. I want what goes on inside my head to be mine, and only mine."

"Point made." Maggie stared at the ceiling. "Hear that? I couldn't agree with Ellen more. If you're listening, ladies, you'd better have gotten the message. Let us handle all this. You two keep out!"

In the computer room Lucy covered her ears with the heels of her hands. "Don't yell. We hear you."

"So you'll leave Ellen's fantasies alone? She's got to grow at her own speed, without your interference. Do I have your promise?"

Lucy sighed. "I suppose, but it's such fun pushing her a bit."

"No pushing," Maggie's voice said. "Not even a little bit."

"Just make it snappy. I want to see progress soon."

"Lucy . . ." Maggie said, her voice rising.

"Okay. No pushing."

"And no asking Angela to do it for you."

"Shit," Lucy snapped, staring at Angela with a guilty expression on her face.

Grinning, Angela said, "She knows you too well, Luce."

"All right, Maggie. I'll leave her alone." She glared at Angela. "Don't call me Luce."

Maggie sighed, then said to Ellen, "Done. They got the message, loud and clear."

"See you tomorrow?"

"Lucy's getting impatient so I'm sure you will."

Ellen watched Maggie open the apartment door, walk through it, and just sort of disappear. Fade away. Slowly the door swung shut and Ellen collapsed on the sofa. Part of her

brain was spinning, trying to put all the pieces of the pre-
ceding few hours together. Part of her couldn't grasp what
had happened, yet another part already missed Maggie's
comforting presence. This was all moving too quickly and
Maggie had said that Lucy was already impatient. She
glanced down and saw the CD still in her hand. What the
hell. In for a penny . . .

CHAPTER 4

Wineglass in hand, Ellen wandered into the bathroom and turned on the taps in the tub. She set up a small, portable CD player that she'd brought from upstate on the toilet seat, poured some bath salts that Micki had given her last Christmas under the rushing water and watched bubbles rise up the sides of the tub. When the water was as high as it could get, she stripped off her clothes, put the CD in the player, and climbed into the hot bath. With a long sigh, she settled beneath the soothing water and sipped her drink.

Why am I hesitating? she asked herself. *Play the thing.* Yet she didn't press the play button. *I'm embarrassed,* she admitted to herself. *I've never read a dirty book or an erotic story before.* Hot scenes in contemporary novels had always excited her, but that was different. She wasn't reading those just for stimulation. And listening? It seemed so personal.

She sipped again, enjoying the slight buzz the wine was causing. Maggie was right about the wine, she thought, so maybe she was right about this. She reached for the player. She could always switch it off. She pressed the button.

"Just After Midnight—A Collection of Erotic Stories by CJ Winterman. Read by the author."

The voice was deep and rich and the music in the background reminded Ellen of saxophones on warm summer evenings. She rested her head against the back of the tub and closed her eyes.

"Is there magic in the world? Skeptics doubt that magic exists, or ever did exist. Are they right? I don't know, but there are still a few people who are willing to keep an open mind, people who believe in old stories, ancient legends, and possibilities. Like the possibilities inherent in the Elixir of Lust.

"Anthony was lost. He was utterly, completely, and totally lost. He had gotten out of the cab at what he thought was an intersection around the corner from his girlfriend's apartment, but as the taxi pulled away he realized that this wasn't the place he had thought it was. He turned, prepared to hail another cab, but there was not one in sight. As a matter of fact, there were almost no cars in sight either.

" 'Okay,' Anthony said out loud, 'I'll just have to find a phone and call a cab or a limo or whatever. Anything to get me to Elaine's in time for dinner.' Elaine was not usually in the best of moods when he was late for one of her infrequent home-cooked meals. 'Shit,' he hissed.

"He looked up and down the street for a store that might have a phone, but in this rundown area, who knew what you would find behind the shabby doors.

Ultimately he selected one at random, between a dilap-idated clothing store and a vacant lot. He peered through the grimy front window and saw a shape mov-ing around inside. 'At least there's someone in there,' he mumbled. He gazed at the sign, letters in Magic Marker on a piece of dingy yellowed cardboard propped in the corner of the window. HARRY'S POTIONS AND NOS-TRUMS. HARRY GAINES, PROP. *Another cardboard sign proclaimed* HOURS 10:00 A.M. *to* 6:00 P.M. WEEKDAYS. *Well, Anthony thought gazing at his watch and seeing that it was just five to six,* it ought to be open.

"*He pushed at the door and, as it swung slowly to admit him, a bell rang. 'I'm closed,' a scratchy voice called.*

" *'It's not six yet,' Anthony said, 'and anyway I just want to use your phone.'*

" *'Closed is closed,' the voice wheezed as a stooped, wizened old man emerged from behind the dusty counter. 'Sorry. Come back tomorrow.'*

" *'I just want to use your phone to call a cab,' An-thony repeated, this time more loudly.*

" *'Phone's only for customers,' the man said, scratch-ing his crotch through his baggy trousers.*

" *'Please. I'll pay you for the use of the phone. I've got to get a cab. If I don't get one soon my ass is toast.'*

" *'Toast?' the man wheezed.*

"*He needed this guy to let him use his phone so An-thony took a deep, calming breath. 'Please. My girl-friend will kill me if I'm late for dinner. She's cooking for me and she gets totally pissed if I'm not there on time.'*

" *'Phone's for customers only,' the man repeated.*

" *'Okay I'll buy something. What do you sell?' At this point it didn't matter much what the guy was selling as* long as it meant that the man would allow him to use the phone.

" 'That's better,' the man said. 'I sell potions, powders, nostrums, all kinds of things that people need. What do you need?'

" 'Need? How about a million dollars and a cab?'

"The man's laugh was brittle and ended in a spasm of coughing. 'A million dollars. That's a good one. You've got a good sense of humor, young man. Now tell me. What do you really need?'

" 'Right now I need to get a cab and a good story to explain to Elaine why I'm late.'

" 'Elaine's your girlfriend, right?'

" 'Going on three months now.'

" 'Do you love her? Does she love you?'

" 'I suppose.' Anthony had had enough of conversation. He would buy whatever the old man offered, within his price range of course. 'Now listen. What can I buy so that I can use the phone?'

" 'I suppose I could sell you a love potion.'

" 'Sure. Right. A love potion. If only it were that simple.'

" 'But it is that simple. I can sell you a love potion, or a lust potion, if you prefer.'

" 'A lust potion?' The old man had certainly gotten his attention with the phrase.

" 'That's what I said. Does that interest you?'

" 'How does this lust potion work?'

" 'The Elixir of Lust is really very straightforward. You put a drop on your finger and touch your girlfriend. Then she lusts after you.' He leaned closer, a wheezy laugh escaping from between his yellowed teeth. 'If you put a drop or two on her pussy, she'll go crazy.'

" 'How much?'

" 'Only twenty dollars for a small vial. Enough for many evenings of delight. In the future, the price might be a bit higher. When you realize the potential of the elixir of course.'

"Anthony was sure that the stuff couldn't possibly work, but if buying some would get the use of the phone, he would do it. 'I'll just take the twenty-dollar vial, and a phone.'

"Several minutes later when the cab was on the way, the man handed him a small vial of yellowish liquid with an old-fashioned cork closing the opening. 'Here's my card, too, young man. Even if you use the Elixir of Lust sparingly, and you should of course, you might want to order more at some point. Just call and I'll have some ready for you to pick up.'

" 'This will be fine,' Anthony said, seeing the cab pull up in front. He stuffed the vial and the business card in his jacket pocket and scurried out.

" 'I can't believe you're late,' Elaine whined as Anthony walked into her kitchen. 'After all the time I took making this lasagna and now it's cold.'

" 'You can put it in the oven and reheat it. I'm sure it will be wonderful.' He reached out to hug her but she twisted away.

" 'It's ruined,' she moaned. 'Ruined.'

" 'Please, baby. Just try.' Anthony picked up the casserole dish and almost burned his hands. 'It's still hot. I think we can just eat it the way it is.' He leaned over the dish and gave an exaggerated sniff. 'It smells sensational.'

" 'The bread will be overdone.'

"Anthony sighed and wondered whether it was all worth it, but when he thought about being alone, no sex, no female company, he swallowed hard. It had been difficult to get Elaine to go out with him in the first place. He was twenty-six and, since he wasn't good with women, she was his first real, steady girlfriend. 'Come on, darling, I know it will be great.'

"She pouted prettily and consented to join him at the small table in her kitchen. They talked pleasantly over lasagna and bread, both wonderfully cooked despite the delay, and sipped some delicious Chianti.

"Later, as they sat on the sofa watching a video, Anthony thought about the small bottle in his jacket pocket. It had cost him twenty bucks. Maybe it would do something. He headed for the bathroom and, on the way back to the TV, got the vial and slipped it into the pocket of his jeans.

"The movie was a sad love story, and, while Anthony found himself bored, Elaine was paying close attention, dabbing her eyes with a tissue. With as little movement as possible, he withdrew and uncorked the tiny bottle, pressed his finger over the opening and tipped the vial. The yellowish oily liquid coated a small area on the pad of his index finger. He put his arm around Elaine.

" 'Come on, baby,' she said. 'This is the best part of the film.'

"He touched the oil to the side of Elaine's neck and stroked his finger down her white skin. When nothing happened immediately Anthony wasn't surprised. Chalk it all up to getting here almost on time and making Elaine happy. Twenty bucks wasn't too high a price to pay.

"For several minutes Anthony merely stared at the TV, bored to tears. 'Baby,' Elaine said suddenly, 'why don't you pay attention to me instead of the movie?'

"Surprised by her sudden shift, Anthony said, 'I thought you were enjoying the film.'

"Elaine's head dropped back onto Anthony's arm. 'Not as much as I would enjoy you,' she purred, turning her lips toward his mouth.

"Anthony leaned over to place a gentle kiss on his girlfriend's pursed lips and, as their mouths touched, Elaine reached out, cupped the back of his head and dragged him closer. She held his head tightly against hers, pressing her tongue between his lips. 'Mmm,' she purred, changing the angle of the kiss to better fit her mouth against his.

"Anthony was stunned. Elaine was usually passive, pliant, willing, but never the aggressor in matters of sex. Tonight, however, she was devouring him. She moved so she was straddling his lap, her hands tugging at his shirt. Could it be the Elixir of Lust? Anthony wondered. Could the stuff really work? What a blast!

"Anthony thought little more about it. Reveling in Elaine's newfound aggression, he tore at her clothes as she dragged his belt from its loops. Soon they were naked, Elaine climbing all over him in an effort to get closer. She pressed his hands to her breasts, then urged him to tweak her nipples. With her head thrown back and her chest pushing against his hands, she panted like an animal in heat.

"Anthony's cock reacted predictably, growing and hardening with Elaine's every movement. As she prepared to mount him he remembered what the wheezy old man had said. 'Put a drop or two on her pussy, she'll go crazy.' He found the vial in his pants pocket and put another drop of the oily liquid on his finger. Then he rubbed his finger over her swollen pussy-flesh, pushing it into her channel.

" 'More,' she screamed. 'Fill me up. Fuck me with your fingers. Do it!' Frantically she bucked against Anthony's hand as he drove two, then three fingers into her. Almost incoherent with lust, she grabbed his wrist, pulled his fingers from her pussy and plunged downward onto his erect shaft. Over and over she raised her hips, then dove onto his pole. Knowing this couldn't last, Anthony thrust upward, meeting her every movement. It was only moments until he erupted, spurting jism deep into her pussy.

"As he panted, he watched Elaine eagerly rub her clit, finally succeeding in bringing herself to a climax of earth-shattering proportions. Together they collapsed onto the sofa and lay there long minutes until their breathing finally calmed. 'Holy mackerel,' Elaine said, stroking his chest, 'I have no idea what came over me, but that was incredible.'

" 'It certainly was,' Anthony said. 'Magnificent.'

"Later that evening, home in bed, Anthony relived the entire experience. It must have been the elixir, he realized. It was difficult to accept but the stuff must have worked, and when he put a drop on her cunt, well she nearly exploded. He found his cock getting hard just thinking about it. I wonder. . . .

"He climbed out of bed and fetched the small vial from his pocket. As he lay back down he uncorked the bottle and again coated his finger. Then he touched the oil to his cock, stroking it along its length.

"The effect was almost instantaneous. Brilliant colors filled his vision. Images of naked women playing with their breasts, tempting him with hugely erect nipples. Pussies of all sizes and shapes, some shaven, some thick with curly pussy hair, thrust toward him, dripping with juices. Fingers stroked the wetness and then coated his lips with it.

"He could feel hands all over his body, stroking his

toes, *his calves, under his arms, between his fingers. Mouths kissed and licked every inch of his body. A tongue—no, several tongues—licked the length of his erection. A hot, wet mouth enveloped his cock, taking the length of it into a dark wet world of erotic sensation.*

"*Without realizing he was doing it, Anthony wrapped his hand around his cock and stroked the length of his shaft. He cupped his balls with the other hand and closed his eyes to better enjoy all the sensations at once. In only moments he came, wads of thick come splashing onto his belly, then he felt nothing more until morning.*

"*As he slowly awoke he recalled the previous evening in detail. One drop on his cock and he had had the best orgasm of his life. Over the next few weeks, he saw Elaine several times, but the frequency diminished. Every night he used the Elixir of Lust on his own cock and found that he didn't need Elaine or anyone else. His fantasies and the yellow oil were enough.*

"*Finally one evening he took out the vial and realized that it was just about empty. He stared at it, rubbing his pinky around the inside to retrieve the last remnants for that evening. Tomorrow, he reasoned, he'd call the man and order more.*

"*The following morning he searched for the business card the old man had handed him. He'd washed the jeans he'd been wearing that day several times since then and the card was nowhere to be found. He turned his room upside down. No card. He even called Elaine and asked her whether the small white card might have fallen out of his pocket, but she hung up on him. He tried the yellow pages and the phone company but got nowhere. He got a cab and roamed the area around*

*Elaine's house looking for the shabby old doorway with
no success.*

*"That was many years ago. It is said that on any
given afternoon a now-aged man named Anthony can
still be found asking everyone on the street whether
they'd ever seen a store called Harry's Potions and Nos-
trums. Good luck, Anthony."*

Ellen roused herself from the stupor she had fallen into and
pushed the stop button on the CD player. With little hesitation she slid her hand down her belly and through the hair
beyond. As she found the slippery folds of her pussy, she
thought about the story she'd just heard. If she were to be
as honest with herself she would have to admit that her fingers felt good rubbing her clit. Faster and faster she rubbed,
circling her clit and sliding over her juicy flesh, feeling the
difference between the water and the fluids that flowed from
her body.

"Oh, God," she moaned as her pleasure grew. Her
breathing quickened, her heart pounded and she wanted. For
the first time she slipped one finger into her channel and, as
her orgasm washed over her she could feel the pulses of her
pussy with her inserted finger. "Oh, God."

She lay in the tub for several more minutes before climbing
out, drying herself with a small white bath towel and sliding
into bed. She fell into a dreamless sleep.

The following morning Ellen awoke, her mind already
churning. Maggie. What did the ghost really want from her?
Did Ellen want great sex? Of course she did, but what did
the phrase *great sex* mean to her? She realized immediately
that she had no idea. She wasn't a virgin. She and Gerry
Swinburn had had a sexual relationship for almost a year
before he moved to New York. It had been all right. After

all it had been her first, and up to now only, sexual experience. They had gradually moved from heavy petting to each rubbing the other to climax to actual intercourse in her parents' living room while they were away. She and Gerry had never spent the night together although they had planned to move in together before his defection.

What did she know about good sex, or even mediocre sex? Did she want to know about all the variations on plain old intercourse? Ellen stretched out beneath the covers and smiled. Yes. She did. Now that she had the opportunity, she accepted that she wanted to know it all. She wanted to enjoy the company of men, in and out of bed. She wanted to feel attractive, like the well put together women she passed on the street each day. She wanted to look sophisticated, classy, like she knew the secrets of the world. She wanted to know those secrets.

Ellen wriggled against the cool sheets and realized that she was naked. The previous evening after her bath she hadn't stopped to put on pajamas, and being naked felt wonderful. Her body felt wonderful, satisfied yet hungry for more. She climbed out of bed and padded into the bathroom, closed the door, and gazed at herself in the full-length mirror. Not bad, she thought. She was a bit overweight with flesh covering her bones and softening her shape but she didn't look flabby. Face? Well, there wasn't anything there that made her cringe.

No. It wasn't her looks that were the problem. A little help with wardrobe and such and her body would pass muster. It was her mind that, as yet, wouldn't get her anywhere in the land of the sexually knowledgeable. She needed an education.

She grabbed the CD player, still sitting on the toilet seat, set it up on her bedside table and climbed back between the sheets. She pressed the play button and the familiar voice began.

"*Is there magic in the world? Skeptics doubt that magic exists, or ever did exist. Are they right? I don't know, but there are still a few people who are willing to keep an open mind, people who believe in old stories, ancient legends, and possibilities. Like the possibilities inherent in the Wine of Willingness.*

"*The bottle was on the bottom shelf of the wine store, covered with dust. Leslie didn't know what teased at her, but she bent down and pulled the heavy bottle from its cubbyhole. 'Hey, Darryn,' she said, 'how about this one for tonight?'*

"*Her husband came up beside her and looked at the old bottle in her hand. 'The Wine of Willingness. What a name! I've never heard of it. It's got no year, no appellation, no nothing. What made you pick that one?'*

"*'I haven't a clue,' Leslie said, 'but it seemed to draw me over.' She rubbed the grime from the back label.* HE WHO DRINKS THIS WILL BE ABLE TO ENJOY PLEASURES BEYOND HIS WILDEST DREAMS, *she read. 'Wow. That's quite a promise.' She grinned at her husband. 'Let's give it a try. What have we got to lose?'*

"*'I'll tell you what we have to lose. This is obviously someone's idea of a kinky game, maybe a gimmick to sell wine. It's probably overpriced swill.' He took the bottle from Leslie's hands and walked to the counter. 'How much?'*

"*The clerk looked the bottle over for the bar code but found none. 'This must be private stock. Let me look the price up for you.' Moments later, after flipping through pages in a large notebook, he said, 'Wine of Willingness. Strange name and I've never seen a bottle before.' He continued to flip pages. 'Ahh. Here it is.' He stared. 'I don't get this price. The book says that any couple, and it specifies a* couple, *who wants a bottle of the Wine of Willingness gets it for nothing. This is really odd but if that's what it says, that's what you get.' He looked at Leslie. 'You his lady?'*

" *'Yes,' she said.*

" *'Well then, I guess there's no charge.'*

" *'Free?' they said in unison.*

"The clerk turned the book so Darryn and Leslie could read the entry. WINE OF WILLINGNESS. ANY COUPLE WHO BRINGS YOU A BOTTLE SHALL BE TOLD THAT IT'S FREE. IT CANNOT, HOWEVER, BE SOLD TO AN UNACCOMPANIED PERSON. 'Do you want to take it?' the clerk asked.*

" *'For nothing? Sure. Why not?'*

"The clerk slipped the wine into a bag and, totally confused, Darryn and Leslie took it home. As they finished preparing dinner, Darryn took out the wine opener. 'I feel like I stole this,' he said.*

" *'I know. That was so weird.'*

"Darryn looked over the label, then rubbed off more grime. 'Wait, it says more.' He read the words, almost obscured by the discolored paper. SIP THIS WINE TOGETHER AND THEN EXPRESS YOUR FONDEST WISH. THE WINE OF WILLINGNESS WILL DO THE REST. This is really nuts.'*

" *'As long as the stuff's not too awful what the heck.'*

"Darryn uncorked the wine and poured two glasses. The liquid was deep ruby red and almost seemed to glow from the depths of the glass. 'It looks wonderful,' Darryn said. He placed the glass near his nose* *and inhaled. 'Wow. It's got a bouquet that won't quit. Fruit, flowers, everything. I hope it tastes as good as the nose.'*

"Leslie took her glass, appreciated the color, then breathed in the deep aroma. 'That's fantastic.' She sipped. 'This is a find, a wonderful full flavor, with so much of everything, earth, fruit, I even taste blackberries and, well, everything.'

"Darryn sipped. 'This is some of the best wine I've ever tasted.'

"Throughout dinner they drank until the bottle was almost empty. Giggling, they stacked the dishes in the sink and walked into the living room, ready to watch TV. 'You know,' Leslie said, 'the bottle said we should each tell our fondest wish.'

" 'That's silly,' Darryn said. 'My fondest wish was that the wine wasn't lousy, and it wasn't. That's that.'

" 'Don't be such a slug,' Leslie chided. 'What's your fondest wish? Really.'

"Darryn settled on the sofa and draped his arm around his wife's shoulders. 'I wish I could make mad, passionate love to you right here and now.'

" 'Why couldn't you?' Leslie had always been a bedroom person, but tonight, with a buzz from the wine, it seemed just fine to do it here in the living room. 'Would you like to make love here on the sofa?'

"Darryn's eyes widened. 'Oh, baby. I've always wanted to love you in every room of the house.'

"Leslie's mind was filled with possibilities. It all sounded so wonderful. 'I never thought about the kitchen, but why not? Sounds deliciously kinky.'

" 'Would you take off your clothes? Right here and now?'

" 'Sure. Would you like to watch?'

"Shit, *Darryn thought,* this isn't happening. My prim, conservative little wife is volunteering? *'Would you strip for me?'*

" *'That sounds perfect.' She stood up, moved the coffee table out of the way, then tuned the radio to a station that specialized in music from the seventies. She started to move her hips to a disco beat, bumping and grinding to the heavy percussion. Her eyes closed, she swayed, slowly unbuttoning her shirt.*

" *'Oh, baby,' Darryn said. 'Go with it.'*

" *'Of course,' she sighed, dragging her shirttails from her jeans. She pulled it off and swung it by one sleeve, windmilling it around until it flew through the air and landed in Darryn's lap. At an agonizingly leisurely pace, she pulled off her shoes, socks, and jeans. Prancing around the living room in only her white cotton bra and panties, she danced to the rhythm. When the song ended she stopped and stared at her husband. 'Do you like me?'*

" *'Oh, God, yes,' he said, unable to believe what he was seeing. His cock was straining at the crotch of his jeans, but he sat still, not wanting to endanger his wife's mood. 'You're so sexy.'*

"Leslie stood between his knees, bent down, and grabbed his erection through his pants. 'Hmm. You certainly do think so. Now it's your turn. You can strip for me.'

" *'Strip? Men don't strip.'* Well, why not? *Darryn thought.* If it makes her as hot as it makes me, what the heck. *As Leslie settled on the couch, Darryn slowly stood and listened to the disco beat of the new song on the radio. He had always hated dancing, but this wasn't dancing exactly; he was putting on a show like those Chippendale guys. He wiggled his hips and was re-*

warded with a heated gaze from his wife. He turned and let her watch him move his ass, bending over so he could look at her between his spread legs. While his back was to her, he opened his shirt and pulled it off.

"As he turned around, she yelled, 'Go for it, hunk.'

"Hunk. Yeah! He mimicked thrusting, driving his hips forward, watching his wife's eyes riveted on his crotch. He quickly pulled off his shoes and socks, then danced around the living room, curling his toes in the carpeting. Why hadn't he noticed before what a sensual thing carpeting was? He danced his way to the couch and pulled Leslie to her feet, pressing his crotch against her mound. Together they sinuously rubbed their bodies together, getting hotter and hotter.

"Do it in every room of the house, Darryn thought. He danced his wife into the kitchen and, with the disco beat pounding in his head, he lifted her onto the counter, pushing canisters and small appliances out of his way. He quickly draped her legs over his shoulders until she was totally open to him with only her white panties covering her.

"He rubbed his finger over her already damp and hot mound, listening to the small cooing noises she made. He watched her close her eyes and let her head drop backward. Darryn spied a jar of jam on the counter and unscrewed the top. Pulling one of Leslie's bra cups to one side, he coated her areola with thick strawberry preserves. As Leslie looked on in amazement, Darryn's long tongue found her, slowly lapping at her erect nipple.

"With one swift motion, Leslie removed her bra and scooped a large dollop of jam onto her finger, using it to coat her other nipple. Darryn feasted on his wife's body, spreading jam and licking until he was ready to rip her panties off and take her right on the counter.

" 'Not yet,' Leslie said, sliding down. She patted the counter and, with a lift of his hip, Darryn slid onto it. Quickly Leslie removed the rest of Darryn's clothes and coated his raging hard-on with jam. As Darryn watched she slowly drew his strawberry-flavored cock into her mouth. Darryn was in heaven, delighted and amazed at his wife's willingness to take him orally, as he'd always wanted her to. As his mind blurred, the phrase the Wine of Willingness whirled in his head.

"With a motion of her head, Leslie urged Darryn from the counter. 'Every room,' she purred. She grabbed his hand, dragged him into the dining room and stretched out on her back on the dining room table. 'Here too,' she growled.

"Darryn realized that the table was just the right height for his cock so he pulled Leslie to the edge, yanked off her panties and plunged his still-sticky cock into her soaked pussy. As he slammed into her, he had to grip her hips to keep her from sliding across the table. 'Yes, yes, yes!' she screamed, louder and louder. 'More! Fuck me! Fuck me hard, now!'

"Darryn kept pounding into her, spurred on by her screams and the needs of his body. Over and over he rammed his cock into her sweet pussy until he could no longer control his body. 'I can't stop it!' he cried and, with a final plunge of his hips, he poured semen deep into his wife.

"She didn't come, Darryn thought as his cock slowly withdrew from his wife's body. 'Do what you need,' he growled. With little hesitation his prim little wife reached between her legs and rubbed her beautiful snatch with her long fingers until, only moments later she slammed her elbows into the table, almost lifting herself off the surface. 'Yes! Oh, God, yes! Now!'

"*Later, curled beside his wife in bed, Darryn said, 'I don't know what came over us, but it was fantastic. Maybe the Wine of Willingness had something to do with it.'*

" 'It's too bad we don't have anymore,' Leslie said, sleepily.

" 'If we agree to be honest with each other, and as free as we were tonight, maybe we don't need any more magic wine.'

" 'We should make a pact. Every bottle of wine will be like the Wine of Willingness.'

" 'And every glass of water, too,' Darryn said and Leslie giggled as they fell asleep."

CHAPTER 5

When Maggie arrived in Ellen's living room an hour later, Maggie was wearing a royal purple silk shirt and a pair of off-white jeans. She had covered the shirt with a white fringed vest and she wore matching cowboy boots.

"You look great," Ellen said, gazing down at her Mickey Mouse sweatshirt, black jeans, and sneakers. "I wish I had your flair for clothes."

"Actually I'm not sure where my clothes come from. They just show up in a dressing room right before I arrive here. I've been doing this for months and I still don't have any idea of how it all works. How was your evening?"

"I listened to the first two stories on the CD and I think I understand what you've been trying to tell me." One of Maggie's dark brows lifted. "I guess I want to find out what's out there," Ellen continued. "I want to date, have some fun, enjoy what life has to offer."

Maggie's grin lit her face. "Your speech is still filled with

'I guess' and 'I think' but so far so good. You're learning that everyone has the right to good things, including great sex, and that sometimes it's necessary to go and get it."

"I think I'm ready to give it a try. Where do we start?"

Maggie gave Ellen a critical once-over. "Clothes, I think, and maybe some time at a salon I know of. Manicure, pedicure, hair, makeup, the works."

"You know, I still catch myself wondering whether I can afford something like that. I guess I'm not used to having the money to do selfish things."

"What I'm suggesting isn't selfish. It's a necessary part of becoming someone new and different. I worked with a woman who didn't have much money. Her makeover consisted of a home permanent with a little new color added, a magazine article on makeup, and a trip to Wal-Mart for cosmetics. We added a new scent, a few inexpensive clothes, and voila. You don't need money."

"I understand, and I do need to feel good about myself and about where I fit. I guess I'm ready. Let's do it."

"What time is it? I can't wear a watch since time has little significance to me." When Ellen looked puzzled, Maggie continued, "Time is a relative thing. For example, it feels to me as if I just left you moments ago, but I know I've got new clothes and, since the sun's shining, I assume that it's morning now. The time in between just seems to disappear. Actually it could be a morning several months after the evening I gave you the CD. I'd never know the difference."

"So how do you know when to arrive? Or do Lucy and Angela make those decisions."

Maggie's brown eyes gazed upward. "Oh, they're in charge all right and they make the decisions. The other women I've worked with tell me that I seem to show up just when I'm needed."

Ellen didn't know whether it was bad manners to probe

too deeply, but her curiosity had gotten the better of her and Maggie seemed willing to answer questions. "Where do you go when you leave here?"

Maggie seemed confused. "I've no idea. Sort of nowhere, I guess. I don't age, my nails and hair don't grow." She ran her fingers through her dark curls. "I don't even need a touch-up. I seem to look the same and feel the same as I did when I . . . died."

Died. Ellen still had a difficult time absorbing the fact that this woman, who seemed more alive than most of the people she knew, was really dead. "When was that?"

"In July of 1995 I had a heart attack in my sleep. All very painless. I went to bed one night and woke up in the computer room with Angela and Lucy."

Ellen glanced at her watch. "It's only eight-thirty. Want coffee? I know you drink wine, but do you eat? I don't usually have breakfast but I can see what I've got if you're hungry."

"Coffee would be nice but I don't usually eat. Sometimes I get hungry or thirsty but most of the time it's sort of nothingness in my stomach."

In the kitchen, Ellen put ground coffee into the top of the maker and poured in cold water. She sat at the tiny table with Maggie across from her. "What's it like? Being dead, I mean."

Maggie propped her elbows on the table. "For me, except for some of the logistics, it's not too different from being alive. I've had some great experiences and met some wonderful people. Strangely enough I enjoy what I'm doing."

Ellen had no concept of what it would be like to be dead and to be bounced around in time the way Maggie was. "Do you mind me asking all these questions? It's just so foreign to me."

"I don't mind. I've asked a few myself and I have to tell you that Lucy and Angela aren't long on sensible answers."

Ellen couldn't suppress a grin. "I'll bet. Tell me about the others you've helped. Without violating confidences, I mean."

Maggie leaned back and stretched her legs beneath the table. "Barbara Enright was the first. She was a wonderful woman, as they all were really. Each one merely needed someone to open them up to the possibilities of good sex, to help them feel good about themselves."

"I feel good about myself," Ellen protested.

"You're a bit different. It's more your outlook. You need to learn to get out there and do things rather than peeking out at the world. You need to get your feet wet, then to soak the rest of you. Dive in. Give things a try."

"I try things," Ellen protested. "I came to the city, didn't I?"

"You came to New York City at the insistence of your sister but once you got here you did nothing to fit in."

"I did lots of things," Ellen snapped. "I've visited most of the places in the city that Micki told me are worthwhile. Museums, art galleries, the top of the World Trade Center, St. Patrick's. I've been everywhere."

"I know you think you have, but did you try anything new, just for you?" Maggie leaned forward and her eyes locked with Ellen's. "Have you been anywhere that Micki didn't suggest? Have you done anything really different, gone to the zoo, Coney Island, or the Bronx Botanical Garden? Have you considered taking a cruise? Visiting Tokyo? Have you tasted sushi? Have you had a massage? Have you bought anything to make this apartment more than a nomad camp? Have you ever done anything daring just because you were curious?"

Ellen sat up straight. "Maybe not, but I like just looking."

"Looking's fine for a while, but now it's time for tasting. Since I know about sex and men, I'm hoping that will be the vehicle to pull you from visiting to living."

"What does sex have to do with living?" When Maggie just raised an eyebrow, Ellen continued, "You know what I mean."

"I'm afraid I do. If I were going to color your world right now I'd have to use pastels. Now it's time for emerald and scarlet, indigo and marigold. Let's be honest. Even your fantasies are insipid, wimpy. What do you really want out of life? Lucy and Angela seem to think they know, but do you?"

Ellen considered. "I always thought I was satisfied with my life. When I won the lottery I thought I'd just do more of what I've always done."

"I know but there's so much more to life than what you've always had. Don't you want to at least sample some of what's out there?"

Ellen slowly settled back in her chair. "You mean like taking that art class."

"You did that at Micki's suggestion but it's a start, a small step in the right direction." Maggie grasped Ellen's hand. "You don't have to dive in, but you're thirty-two. It's time for getting your feet wet in the immense ocean of what there is."

"If you say so."

"No, not because I say so, because you're curious and because you're feeling just a little bit braver than you did yesterday."

"That little old chicken, me."

"You don't have to do everything at once, and I'll be there to hold your hand, figuratively, if not literally."

"Maybe you're right. Maybe it's time to live a little." She held her thumb and index finger about a half an inch apart. "Just a little to start."

"That's fine. We'll take it just a bit at a time and I'll help all I can."

"Thanks. Will that be enough for you? Enough to make Lucy and Angela happy?"

"Forget about all of us. This is your life, as Ralph Edwards used to say. We're just here to give it a little kick."

"That sounds okay. May I ask you a personal question?"

"Sure. Shoot."

"How did you start? Being a call girl, I mean." She gulped. "I'm sorry. I mean . . ."

Maggie's eyes held nothing but warmth. "Stop falling over your words. They're only words. I was a hooker. I had sex with men for money and I enjoyed it."

"But prostitution . . ."

"Prostitution is such a charged word with all kinds of overtones. Let's just say this. I loved good sex, and so did most of the men I was with.

"Most of the men?"

"You know it's interesting. Some wanted companionship, someone to be with and there wasn't any sex at all. Just a nice decoration for a party or dinner or someone to talk to who had no other issues."

"No sex at all?"

"There were a few times like that when some longtime client just wanted to be with someone who didn't want anything from him." Her impish grin brought a smile to Ellen's face. "Of course there were others who wanted something unusual, something they couldn't get with anyone they didn't pay. Something fun and kinky."

"I guess you had to do all kinds of kinky stuff."

"I did, and I had a heck of a lot of fun too. If it's not fun for both parties, it's not fun for either."

"Weren't there men who just wanted to, well, fuck." Heat rose in Ellen's face at the use of such a four-letter word.

"If they just wanted to insert tab A into slot B they didn't have to pay my kind of money. A clean, hundred-dollar-an-hour call girl would do the trick."

"You charged more?" Ellen said, her eyes wide.

"Lots more. I charged between seven hundred and a thousand dollars a night."

"Phew. I never imagined. Were any of the men you were with married?"

"Of course. Many were. Most of the married men I spent time with thought their wives wouldn't want to do the things we did together. I think they were probably wrong, but after one or two protests that they should communicate their desires with their spouses, I gave up and we played."

"You think their wives would have been interested in kinky games?"

"Sure, why not? Listen, we've got to get a few things straight if we're going to have fun learning together. Your expression tells it all." Ellen became aware that her face was registering her disbelief and her distaste. Maggie squeezed her hands. "Listen and try to open your mind. There are many ways to share good sex, ones you've probably never even considered: oral sex, anal sex, toys, bondage. If two consenting adults want to do it upside down, hanging from the crossbar of the kids' swing set, what's wrong with that?"

Ellen sighed. "I guess."

Maggie stood and took two mugs from the counter and filled them with strong coffee. She inhaled. "I love the smell of freshly brewed coffee. What do you take? Milk? Sugar?"

"Black's fine."

"Me, too." Maggie brought the cups to the table and sat back down. "You're limited by the fact that you've never had mind-altering, toe-curling, fan-flippin'-tastic sex."

"Hey, now, wait."

"It's true, whether you admit it or not."

"I've had sex."

"I know. With that Gerry character. He was a nice guy but a lightweight."

"You know about Gerry?"

"I know everything about you." When Ellen started to respond, Maggie held up her hand. "Almost everything, and I'm sorry that Angela and Lucy pry. It's just their way." She sipped the hot brew. "I don't mean mediocre sex with Gerry, nice as he was. I mean climaxes when you've screamed, begged for more, literally felt like your orgasm should have registered on the Richter scale. When you've felt like it would go on forever, but it was over in an instant, then we'll talk about what's kinky."

"I'm sorry." She thought about Gerry. The sex with him had been fine. Comfortable.

"Comfortable. Right. A mediocre experience at best."

"I wish you'd stop reading my mind."

Maggie looked contrite. "My turn to be sorry. I don't really read your mind, it's just that some of your thoughts are so loud I can hear them. Think about it. Comfortable sex. Sweatshirts and old slippers are comfortable. Sex should be more than just satisfying."

"Was your sex always . . . how did you put it? Mind-altering and toe-curling?"

"Of course not. I don't mean that it has to be earth-shattering every time, but at least now and then it should make you scream. Mine? Well sometimes it was wonderful. Sometimes it was what my friends—I always liked that word better than clients or customers—wanted and I had to get my pleasure from their pleasure."

"What was the best one?"

Maggie sighed. "That's a really tough question. So many

of my friends were wonderful and enjoyed our mutual pleasure. We did things that blew all of our socks off."

Ellen giggled. "Sounds wonderful. Your worst?"

"A few times I had to give a man his money back because
I wouldn't do what he wanted."

"Like?"

"I'm not into pain. Whips and things."

Ellen's lip curled. "That's disgusting anyway."

"No, it's not. It's terribly exciting for many people and
for them it's a sexual turn-on. It's just not one for me and I
decided early on that I wouldn't do things just for money."

Ellen tried to wrap her mind around people wanting to be
whipped. "You wouldn't hit someone if they wanted it?"

"Oh, the occasional slap on the ass is great. It adds a touch
of a different kind of spice. I just couldn't go further. Or,
rather, I didn't want to."

"You never did anything you didn't want to do?"

Maggie twirled a strand of black, curly hair around her
finger as she considered. "I never needed money that badly.
I guess I was pretty fortunate."

"Did you ever get into trouble with the law?"

"No, I never did. I was on my own, no partners, no pimp.
I didn't need anyone else, I had great word of mouth. And
I didn't get into situations I had the slightest doubts about."

"What kind of kinky things did you do?"

"Curious?"

Ellen blushed slightly. "I've read about unusual sex in novels and such, but I've never talked frankly to anyone who
has done anything."

"It's fine to be curious. If I have my way, by the time I'm
done with you you'll have tasted lots of 'unusual' things."
Maggie's eyes became distant. "I really enjoy oral sex, both
giving and getting. Anal sex took a bit of getting used to but
once you get past the taboos, it's really hot. I've made love

in some really strange places and I've done it with several people at the same time."

Ellen sat up straighter. "You did? You were part of an orgy?"

"Sure. Why not?" Maggie stared at Ellen. "Dying of curiosity?"

Ruefully, Ellen nodded. "Okay. I admit it."

"I remember one evening. We were all a bit tipsy, not too drunk to know what we were doing of course, but just enough to release our inhibitions and let it all hang out. That was one hell of a great evening."

"Wow. Would you tell me?"

"Sure. I've got no secrets. I'll use just first names to protect the delightfully guilty."

Ellen refilled the empty coffee cups and sat back down. "Okay. Give."

"Josh was a regular. He traveled a lot on business and usually called me when he was in town. One day he phoned and asked me if I wanted to go to a party. He made it clear that there would be lots of public sex, but that I wouldn't have to participate if I didn't want to."

"You mean he would pay you to just watch? To go to a party with him? Why?"

"He had no one special and it was a badge of honor to bring someone who's not hesitant to play. I have a feeling that several of the women, and maybe the men too, were professionals."

Ellen was shocked. "The men? Professionals?"

"Sure. There are male prostitutes who cater to the desires of sexy, horny women. Why not?"

"I guess I never thought about it that way." Ellen wondered what she would do with a male prostitute and sadly realized that she had no idea what she would ask for."

"You'll learn," Maggie said softly. "I promise."

Ellen reached out and placed her hand over Maggie's on the small kitchen table. "Thanks. Just be patient with me."

Maggie nodded. "No problem."

"Okay. Tell me about the party."

"Josh knew me pretty well. He knew that, although I wouldn't be compelled to do anything, I wouldn't have a problem making love while someone else watched and that was the idea of this party. We'd done it in public a few times."

"In public?"

"Well sort of. He liked to go out to dinner and see how hot he could get me. He knew if he got me hot, I'd do it in a hansom cab, in a restaurant with a few waiters watching, at the beach. You get the idea. So he knew that that part of it wouldn't be a problem. He also knew I was usually game for almost anything. He knew my rules. No drugs, and condoms always.

"Josh is . . . was . . . probably still is . . . I hate trying to make sense of the tenses. Josh was a very good-looking man, tall with really curly chestnut hair that I loved to run my fingers through, and deep hazel eyes. He had a nice body that had added a few pounds over the years I knew him. With the amount of traveling he did, he wasn't able to work out and control it so he always referred to our sex as exercise. 'Just for health reasons,' he'd say." She looked at Ellen and Ellen watched her face soften at the memory. "Then he'd pat his spare tire and grin."

"Was he a good lover?"

"He was a great communicator and experimenter. He loved to try new things. I have a theory. There aren't really any good lovers; there are merely people who are great together, and maybe they wouldn't be nearly as good with other partners. We were marvelous together."

"Interesting," Ellen said, not sure she believed. Could she

be a good lover? Would someone ever say that they were marvelous together?

"We arrived at a small, neat, suburban-looking house in Brooklyn about nine and the party was in full swing. The music was dreamy and Josh and I did a bit of slow-dancing." Maggie closed her eyes again. "I love slow-dancing, vertical body rubbing. I could feel that the atmosphere and the delicious Long Island iced teas we were consuming were having an effect on his libido."

"What were you wearing?"

"I had an amazing blouse that I loved to wear. It was sleeveless, made of a silky red fabric that clung to my breasts and clearly showed my nipples. From the front it had a rather demure neckline, a V with just a hint of cleavage. The interesting part was the back. There wasn't one, just a few strings that tied over my shoulder blades and that was it down to the waist. From the front I was Suzie schoolteacher and from the back I was almost naked."

"Sounds fabulous."

Maggie smiled at the memory. "It was. I wore it with a very short black skirt, five-inch black heels, and thigh-high black stockings. You could just see the lacy tops below the skirt. Josh was wearing black jeans with a yellow cotton shirt."

When Maggie seemed to get lost in the obviously wonderful memories, Ellen said, "So you did some slow-dancing."

"Right. After a few dances, other men began to cut in and I danced with some really nice guys. About an hour after we got there one of the men asked me if I was interested in going in the large hot tub in the basement. It sounded great so I suggested it to Josh. Soon we were downstairs and the joint was jumping. The downstairs was decorated like a forest clearing, with lots of huge split-leaf philodendrons and ficus.

Huge drooping ferns and flowering jungly plants hung from baskets all around the room and the air was wet and heavy and smelled of herbs and earth.

"The center of the room was dominated by a twelve-person hot tub with a wide ledge around it that, in addition to couples draped over one another, held pitchers of frozen drinks and trays of munchies. Two couples lay on the ledge beneath heat lamps, hands and mouths busy. At that moment the tub contained eight or nine people, all naked, as I quickly found out. 'Wanna get naked and dive in?' Josh growled in my ear, his hot breath making me shiver.

" 'Sure,' I said, kicking off my shoes. Being naked in public has never bothered me."

"I'm sure that's true," Ellen said, "but I'm sure you look great without your clothes."

"Some women look better than others nude but that doesn't make as much difference as you might think. At that party there were four women in the tub. Two had nice figures, one was about fifty pounds overweight, with pendulous breasts and tremendous thighs, and the fourth was really skinny, with almost no breasts at all, just nipples on her ribs. However, everyone had a great time and once the initial gawking subsided, we all had an equal amount of fun. It's mostly mental attitude."

Ellen reflexively looked down. "But that initial impression makes so much difference."

"Does it? And are you really interested in the kind of man to whom that matters so much?"

Ellen sat silent. She realized that what Maggie said made sense, but in her heart she vehemently disagreed. It might be okay for Maggie, who looked really good, but not for her. "So you just stripped?"

"Actually Josh knelt at my feet and slowly peeled my stockings down my legs while several people watched. He deliberately slid his fingers down the inside of my thighs. I have to tell you that that drives me wild. Then he slid off my skirt and kissed my belly over my tiny bikini panties. 'Turn around,' he said, and I did. He untied the strings that held the blouse together and it fell to the floor."

"You, of course, had nothing beneath," Ellen said, with a clear idea of what Maggie must have looked like. Maggie was obviously no kid, but she looked really good despite her age.

Maggie winked. "Of course not. I sag a bit and wish I had more natural uplift, but what the hell. Josh liked me just the way I was, which was obvious when he turned me around and nibbled my nipples. I'm a sucker for that and Josh knew it. He always knew just what made my knees weak and my pussy wet."

Ellen tried not to be startled by Maggie's choice of words.

Maggie's eyes flew open. "Sorry for my language. In my line of work I tend to be rather straightforward. Does it bother you?"

"It's a bit of a surprise coming from you."

"Remember what I did for a living."

"I know, but you look so . . . classy."

"Thanks for the compliment." Maggie closed her eyes again and returned to that night. "So anyway, Josh stripped and we climbed into the tub. The water was wonderful, hot enough to make an impression but not so hot that it muted the ability. I settled beneath the bubbles between Josh and another man. The other man was soft and paunchy, with deep blue eyes behind coke-bottle glasses, which he frequently had to slosh through the hot water to unfog. While we talked I felt hands on my breasts, both Josh's and this other guys."

"He just touched you without permission?"

"Everyone had tacit permission to do whatever they

wanted. I knew that if I had asked him to stop he would have but I didn't because it felt so good. I was getting really hot and it was getting more and more difficult to carry on a coherent conversation. The man looked at Josh who nodded, giving his permission for whatever he wanted to do. 'I'd like to do everything with you.' He was breathing heavily. 'Whatever you like,' I said and almost immediately his fingers were between my legs. God he had great hands.''

As Maggie relived the experience she wondered how much Ellen was ready for. She had reached for the man's cock beneath the bubbling water. It had been soft. "Don't underestimate Junior there," he had said. "All this hot water poops him out, but he recovers quickly."

"I'm glad," Maggie said. "I would hate to be the only one here getting excited."

"Oh, you're not," the two men said almost simultaneously. "Why don't you sit up here?" the man said, patting the wooden ledge. Maggie hoisted herself from the tub and seated herself on the edge. Each man touched a knee and urged her legs apart. While Josh sucked on one of Maggie's breasts, the other man crouched between her legs. "God, you're so juicy. I love a sweet pussy like yours." He slid one finger through her folds and Maggie braced her hands and allowed her head to fall back, savoring the feeling of being pleasured by the two men. Soon she felt the finger slide into her channel, almost immediately followed by another.

"Oh, God, that feels good," she moaned, almost unable to catch her breath as a third finger joined the other two. Josh nipped at one engorged nipple and pinched the other hard. At her gasp, the two men laughed.

"She's a hot number," the man said to Josh. "My name's Al by the way. I guess we should at least know who we are as we play with this hot little piece."

"Her name's Maggie and she's as hot as they come." Maggie heard Josh's rough laugh. "And she does come."

"I'll bet," Al said as he thrust his fingers in and out of Maggie's dripping pussy.

Josh climbed out of the tub and Maggie stretched back onto the ledge. Josh crouched beside her and rubbed his cock against her cheek. When it became erect he growled, "Take it all, baby."

Maggie opened her mouth and it was quickly filled with Josh's erection. She always loved the feel and the taste of him and used her tongue to give him as much pleasure as she could. She soon found it difficult to concentrate, however, as Al's mouth found her clit and licked and sucked her flesh.

Too soon Maggie felt the waves of orgasm washing over her body and, as the spasms controlled her, she felt Josh's cock erupt in her mouth. She tasted his tangy come and swallowed, trying not to allow any to flow out of her mouth.

"Oh, Maggie, you're so sweet," Al said. "I want to fuck you so bad."

Her voice ragged, she said, "If you've got protection."

"I always come prepared." He obviously enjoyed sex immensely and his laugh was infectious. "And I'm always prepared to come."

Maggie heard the familiar sound of ripping foil and then her cunt was filled. "You feel so good," she said as his thrusts drove her upward toward a second orgasm.

Josh idly played with her nipples as Al drove his cock into her again and again. As Al threw his head back and rammed into her one final time, Josh pinched both her nipples and she came again.

Maggie returned to the present, opened her eyes and gazed at Ellen. "I don't think you're ready for the gory details just yet so let's just say that I got enormous pleasure from his fingers inside me and from his magnificent mouth and tongue. When Josh climbed onto the ledge I indulged in my love of fellatio while the other guy fucked me senseless. What a kick. Two men spurting at almost the same time, one in my mouth and one inside my pussy. It was great."

"Wow," Ellen said, her mind whirling. It wasn't just what Maggie had done, it was also her comfort level with it all. She made no excuses and Ellen realized that none were necessary. She obviously had delighted in it all. Listening to Maggie, Ellen was understanding more and more. "It sounds like quite an evening."

"Actually there was a lot more," Maggie said, "but I'll bet it's late enough to get going."

Ellen looked at her watch. "Holy cow. It's after ten."

Maggie grabbed the two cups and put them in the sink. "Let's do it."

"Where do we begin?"

"Let's see whether we can get you an appointment with a new stylist I found on my last assignment." She gave Ellen the phone number. "Ask for Ashley. She's a whiz with hair and makeup." When, due to a fortunate cancellation, Ellen had gotten an appointment for that afternoon, Maggie continued, "I think we should start with clothes."

"What are we buying?" Ellen asked, wondering in what way her wardrobe was insufficient.

"We're getting you a few things that make you feel like the woman I think you can become, a combination of worldly and curious."

"Worldly and curious. Can clothes say that?"

"It's the attitude that matters more than the wrapping but some new duds will certainly help." Maggie grabbed Ellen's purse and tossed it to her. "Let's do some really serious damage to your credit card."

"Okay. You're the boss."

"One thing," Maggie said, grabbing her jacket. "Remember that you're the only one who can see or hear me. Be a bit careful or you'll end up at Bellevue for observation."

Ellen laughed. "Will do."

Chapter 6

Ellen and Maggie walked out into the crisp early fall air of Manhattan. They wandered past shop windows that displayed clothes of all kinds. Each time Ellen indicated something she liked, Maggie sneered. *Wimpy* and *pastel* became her favorite words. Finally they stopped outside a small boutique in the East Sixties. "I used to shop here often when I was alive," Maggie said. "Great stuff." She pushed open the door and Ellen hurried in behind her.

"Good morning, madam," a woman said as she stepped out from behind a rack of blouses. It was all Ellen could do not to gasp. The woman looked to be in her late sixties, with marshmallow-white hair and pale blue eyes. It was obvious that she had been a startlingly beautiful woman and even now she was stunning. Her attire, on the other hand, bordered on bizarre. She was wearing a chartreuse cotton jacket with the sleeves pushed up to her elbows over a cinnamon-and-teal patterned blouse and tailored red slacks. Ellen looked down and found herself staring at a pair of iridescent green sneakers. The woman lifted one foot and wiggled it at the ankle. "Don't you just love them?" she said. "I have tennis shoes to go with almost every outfit. I think it's just too kicky."

"I guess I should have warned you about Flora," Maggie said. "She's a character and her mode of dress certainly is bizarre, but she's got a great eye for style on other people."

"Can I show you something specific or are you just browsing?" Flora asked.

"Well, Flora, I'm just looking for now."

Flora's head snapped around. "How did you know my name?"

"Oh," Ellen said, realizing her mistake. "I had a friend who used to shop here. When I found myself in town, I thought I'd drop in."

"Oh yes? It's nice to have someone recommend my little establishment. What is your friend's name?"

"Her name's Maggie. I mean her name was Maggie."

"Oh, Maggie Sullivan. One of my best customers. What a tragedy. She was so young when she died."

Ellen gazed at Maggie whose expression was unreadable. "Yes, it was, wasn't it." It was so hard to reconcile the Maggie who stood beside her with the woman who had died four years before. Without realizing how awkward the moment was, Flora bustled to a rack of dresses. "I know you said you were just looking, but can I direct you to something more specific? Dresses, suits, blouses? You're a size twelve, aren't you?"

"Yes, a twelve." Soto voce she asked Maggie, "What am I looking for?"

"Anything that's not insipid."

"I can't tell her that."

"Just look around and I'll tell you what to try on."

To Flora, Ellen said, "I'm looking for something new and different from what I usually wear."

"And what is that, if I may ask?"

She considered only a moment. "Well, my friends tell me I'm too pastel, that I need bright colors and some bold prints."

"Bravo!" Maggie said, loudly.

"With your coloring, something bright should look really great. Let's see what I've got."

In just a few minutes, Flora and Maggie had helped Ellen select several looks, each totally different from anything Ellen had ever worn. "I don't know whether I can do this," Ellen said, walking out of the shop's dressing room in a pair of bright red slacks with a white shirt with a wide red stripe and a gold vest. The outfit was held together with a red, gold, and white scarf artfully tied around her throat. "Wonderful," Flora and Maggie said in unison.

For almost an hour, Ellen tried on dresses, pantsuits, and blouses until she had five outfits set aside. She changed back into the first pants ensemble and, in a daze, fumbled in her purse for her wallet. As she pulled out her credit card, Flora said, "If you'll pardon me for saying it, you really need at least one pair of shoes and a matching bag to go with all this."

"You need new underwear, too," Maggie said. "Enough K-mart specials."

Ellen glared at Maggie who had kept up a running conversation, making it difficult for Ellen to respond without appearing to talk to thin air. "I know," Ellen said to Flora and Maggie simultaneously. "I feel like an old house. You change one thing, recover one chair, and everything else looks shabby."

"You don't look shabby at all," Flora said. "You look bright, shiny, and new. Very chic. And remember that everything you've gotten is a classic. With different accessories, they each will last for years. Very practical."

Ellen grinned. "Thanks. It will all take a bit of getting used to."

"You think this is something," Maggie said, "just you wait until Ashley gets her hands and scissors on you."

Maggie accompanied Ellen to Michael's, an exclusive-looking salon in the theater district. The interior was all done in red-and-black patchwork, with black sinks and chairs and operators dressed in patchwork smocks and black pants. "I have an appointment with Ashley," Ellen said to the receptionist, a seemingly natural blonde with a perfect face that couldn't be re-created by any means except the right genes.

"You're Ellen, of course. Ashley will be right with you. Can I take your packages?" She put Ellen's packages in a locker, hung up her new vest, then pressed a hidden button. It was only a moment before a tall, slender woman appeared in the salon uniform.

"Look at Ashley," Maggie said as the woman in her mid-thirties approached. "She's not a particularly attractive woman, but she's a whiz with makeup and she's done her hair in a style that brings out her best features. That's what we want for you."

Ashley smiled and held out her hand. "Welcome. Follow me."

Ellen shook the woman's hand, then followed Ashley to an operator's station and settled into the chair. "Okay," Ashley said, "what can I do for you?"

"I'm not really sure," Ellen said, ruefully. "I just got some new clothes and I guess I want to look worthy of them."

"Okay," Ashley said studying Ellen's face in the mirror. "Do you have anything specific in mind? Cut? Curl? Color?"

"I'm honest enough with myself to admit that I'm not an attractive woman. I guess I didn't pick my parents too well.

I don't know what you can do with what I've got to work with."

"Okay. Let's take a look." Ashley ran her fingers through Ellen's fine hair and rubbed a strand between her fingers. Then she lifted Ellen's chin and moved it left and right, staring critically at her face. "Good bones. I love the green eyes with your ivory skin. Difficult hair as it is now, very straight and very fine, but we can work with that. Small nose, generous, quite sexy mouth."

Ellen stared in the mirror at her mouth. It was just an ordinary mouth with ordinary lips. "Sexy mouth?"

"That slightly pouty lower lip is great. I would use a slightly lighter color lipstick in the center of your lower lip than you use on the rest of your mouth."

"Really?" Ellen asked, still staring.

Ashley seemed not to have heard. "I would go dangling earrings. Your face can't take big round ones but slender hanging ones will accentuate your cheekbones." She peered at Ellen's face and hair then crossed her arms and leaned against the counter. "How brave are you?"

"Very!" Maggie yelled from behind Ellen's chair.

"Not very I'm afraid," Ellen said.

"Ellen," Maggie warned, "you promised."

"I did not," Ellen said.

"Excuse me?" Ashley said, obviously puzzled by Ellen's comment.

"Nothing. What would you suggest?"

"If you're feeling brave, I would go darker with the hair. Deep brown to show off your skin and eyes."

"Darker?"

"Yup. I would also give it a slight body wave and cut it short so it surrounds your face, but doesn't bury it." She got a hairstyle magazine and found a picture of the style she had in mind. "It won't be a dramatic change and I promise that it won't make you uncomfortable. You'll just look like a well retouched picture of yourself."

"Really?"

"I don't think you're ready for something too ultra, if you know what I mean. Let's keep this gentle, a small step for starters. You can always get more-so the next time."

Ellen gazed at the model's picture in the magazine. She was beautiful, but she also had a look, like she understood it all. "That's the look you're after," Maggie said. "That confidence. I think Ashley's right. No drastic changes, just enhancements and a new attitude that can only come when you're happier about yourself."

Not knowing that Maggie was talking, Ashley picked up one of Ellen's hands. "One more thing. You really must get a hand-spa treatment and then have your nails done. I'd recommend wraps in this climate."

"Wraps? Claws?"

"Not at all. I would suggest what we call street-length just over the tips of your fingers. With maybe a soft mauve polish but we've got more than a hundred shades to choose from."

"Say yes, Ellen," Maggie said. "Just say yes."

"I guess," Ellen gulped.

"Hair and nails?" Ashley asked.

Maggie raised her ever-ready eyebrow and Ellen took a deep breath. "Hair and nails."

Maggie squeezed Ellen's shoulder. "Good girl. You'll be glad you did. I promise."

"Right."

"Right," Ashley said, a bit puzzled.

Maggie waved to Ellen and, as she watched, her friend faded away. Her friend. Ellen realized that, in just a few hours, Maggie had become just that. A friend. It still shocked her to see the evidence of Maggie's ghostly existence but she was rapidly getting used to it, or as used to it as she could.

Several hours later, Ellen was gazing at her new look when she saw Maggie slowly reappear. "Wow," Maggie said. "You look fantastic. Ashley was right. You look like you've just come back from a long vacation. The hair's perfect."

"Yeah," Ellen whispered. "It is, isn't it." Ellen had been staring at her reflection in the long mirror for several minutes. She wasn't beautiful. Far from it. But she was classy. Stylish. She looked put together somehow. Ashley had darkened her hair until it was the color of ranch mink and cut and shaped it until it lay sleek against her jaw. She had also used her makeup skills to highlight Ellen's cheekbones and bring out her deep green eyes. As Ellen stared she had to admit that with the way Ashley had done her lipstick she did have a sexy lower lip. "Ellen," Maggie said, "you look sensational."

"Yeah," Ellen breathed. She held up her hands, short, slender fingers tipped with comfortable-length soft mauve nails. "Yeah." For the second time that day Ellen pulled out her credit card without worrying about how much she was charging.

On the way home, Maggie and Ellen stopped at a shoe store and selected several new pairs of pumps and three new pocketbooks to match. Then, just when Ellen thought they were done and that she was juggling as many packages as she could carry, Maggie dragged her into a leather shop and over to a rack of buttery soft cream-colored leather vests with brown bone buttons. She pointed to one. "Try that on. I think it will look great over most of what you've just bought."

Ellen had long since given up arguing, so she stacked her purchases on a bench, slipped off her yellow vest and slid her arms into the leather one. "Oh. This feels so good," Ellen purred, rubbing her hand up and down the front.

From behind her, a low-pitched male voice said softly, "Yes, it does, doesn't it. It looks like it was made for you."

Ellen blushed and said nothing, assuming the voice came from a store clerk. "I'll think about it." She looked at the price tag and blanched. She really liked the vest, but she wasn't going to get shilled by some fast-talking salesman, although, if he worked on commission, she didn't blame him for trying to talk her into buying it.

"Your choice of course," the man said, "but I think you should take it." He moved from behind a rack of jackets. He appeared to be in his mid-thirties, with deep brown eyes, sandy, sun-streaked hair that he wore pulled back in a short tail and a long, sandy mustache. His rugged, not-really-handsome face was deeply tanned, as though he spent quite a bit of time in the sun. No, Ellen thought, not handsome, but friendly and warm, attractive in its openness. Over his tan slacks and plaid sport shirt, he was wearing a brown leather jacket with brass buttons. "Now that you've heard my opinion, I'd like yours. What do you think of this jacket?" It was cut like a sports jacket, but fashioned of deep tan leather that was as soft as fabric. "It's a bit pricey but I really like it. Should I take it?" He turned so she could see the back and sides.

Ellen was nonplussed. "You're thinking of *buying* it?"

Her confusion must have shown on her face because he said, "You don't like it." He slipped the jacket off and started toward the rack from which he had obviously taken it.

"Actually, I do like it. It's really quite becoming." She fumbled for words. "I'm sorry. I thought you worked here and were trying to talk me into purchasing something."

His sudden smile made his face even more attractive. "Oh. I get it. No, I don't work here. I have been gazing at this jacket in the window for weeks and I finally decided to come inside and try it on." He slipped it back onto his shoulders. "You really like it?"

"Yes, I do."

"At these prices, it should come with two pairs of pants. I almost dropped when I saw the cost, but what the heck. You only live once. I just got a bonus and I thought I'd treat myself." He stopped talking. "Sorry. I'm rambling."

"Not at all. And you're right. You do only live once. I'm going to buy this vest and I think you should get the jacket."

He looked at the price tag again, then shrugged. "I'm glad you're getting that vest. It suits you."

"Thanks." Ellen struggled to find something to say as the man slipped the jacket off, draped it over his arm and walked toward the cash register.

Maggie chimed in, "This is your chance to try out the new you. Keep him talking. He's really cute."

"What should I say?" she whispered.

"How about asking his name?"

Ellen trailed after the man, fumbling in her purse for her wallet. "What's your name?" Ellen blurted out, then blanched.

The man's smile was bright. "I'm Jim Lucas. And yours?"

"Ellen. Ellen Harold." She slipped the vest off. "Thanks for the advice." He pulled out a credit card and it was only moments before the transaction was completed and he had the jacket in a box under his arm. As he walked away, Ellen found her credit card and gave it to the salesclerk, then, while he was ringing up the sale, she gathered her shopping bags.

"Ellen," Jim called.

Swallowing, Ellen turned and said, "Yes?"

"Don't forget this," he said, holding the bright yellow vest she had left draped over the rack.

"Oh yeah, thanks again." She stuffed the vest he handed her in one of her shopping bags, then signed the credit-card receipt. Leaving the store, Jim held the door for her. "I live just around the corner, so if you live in the area, maybe we'll run into each other again."

"Maybe we will," Ellen said, moving so Maggie could exit the store behind her. As Jim turned south, Ellen turned north.

"Just great," Maggie said as they approached Ellen's building, her voice dripping with sarcasm. "A cute, sexy guy tries to pick you up and what do you do? Nothing. Not a damn thing. So much for the new you."

"I couldn't let him pick me up. It's not right. It's not safe. He could have been a creep, a thief, a molester."

"Right. And he could have been a millionaire, a diplomat, who knows. You could have encouraged him a bit. You didn't have to invite him to your apartment, but you could have made conversation. Maybe he would have asked you out for a drink."

"Maggie, new me or old me, I'm not that kind of girl. I don't let men pick me up."

Maggie sighed and threw up her hands. "Okay, okay. I hear you. I'll be patient. You'll come around."

"Maybe I won't ever be the kind of woman you have in mind," Ellen said, opening the front door of her building.

"Listen, I'm sorry, love. I didn't mean to snap at you. You're right. You can only be who you are. I know there's someone really special under all that insecurity, and I'm just impatient for you to try your wings."

"Maybe there isn't," Ellen said, stopping at the foot of the stairs, her shoulders slumped. "Maybe I'm just the same old me with a new hairdo. New paint doesn't make the basic structure any different."

"I know it's been only twenty-four hours, but I think I already know you pretty well. The more adventurous you is in there somewhere. I'll relax and stop pushing."

"Thanks. I wish I were as sure of me as you are."

"I understand and on that note, I'll leave you for tonight. You look tired and the day's been full of changes and you need time to adjust, get used to the new you, at least on the outside. I'll see you, well I don't know exactly when I'll see you again, but it will be soon. I'll be around."

As Maggie faded into the stygian darkness that always preceded her periods of inactivity, she could hear voices in her mind. "She's going to be a tough case," she heard Lucy say. "You've got your work cut out for you."

"And it's not just sex, Maggie," Angela's voice added. "You've got to get her to understand about being a woman. About getting involved in the world, not just peeking out at it."

"I know, ladies," Maggie muttered. "I know."

The following morning, Ellen received her weekly package from the doctors in Fairmont and for two days she dutifully coded and entered the data into her computer. Finally she uploaded the completed information to the medical database and e-mailed the files to the doctor's office.

Saturday Ellen wore one of her new outfits as she wandered around Manhattan, trying to feel confident, assured, and classy, with limited success. She looked around her with a more open mind, aware that there were things in New York that she wanted to try that she hadn't previously thought about because Micki hadn't mentioned them. She made a mental note to find out the schedule of the ferry to the Statue of Liberty and the one to the renovated Ellis Island. They were both touristy places to visit, but she was, after all, a tourist and she was curious.

Finding herself at the Hudson River, she decided to visit the Air and Space Museum and found herself fascinated by the military hardware on display. Late in the afternoon, as she walked east, she felt her stomach rumble. As she approached her building, she spotted a small Indian restaurant. She heard Maggie's voice asking, 'Have you ever done anything daring, just because you were curious?' She had never tried Indian food, always afraid it would be too spicy, but today, she stopped and gazed at the posted menu. "I have no idea what most of this stuff is," she muttered.

"Then maybe I can help you," a familiar voice said.

She whirled around and saw the man whom she had encountered in the leather shop. Today he was wearing black jeans, a black shirt, and the tan leather jacket she remembered from the store. He wore high-heeled intricately tooled black cowboy boots so he was several inches taller than she was. "I'm sorry?" He was quite nice-looking and shouldn't have made her nervous, she thought, but he did.

"You said you know nothing about Indian food," he said. "I come here often and I was just stopping here for dinner myself. I thought that maybe, if you were alone, I could join you and help you with the menu."

"I'm afraid I'm on my way somewhere."

"Now I'm the one who's sorry. I took your advice and bought this jacket, now I thought you could take mine and enjoy Indian food. I'm Jim. Jim Lucas." He held out his hand.

"I remember," Ellen said, flustered and blushing slightly. "I'm Ellen." She shook his soft, uncallused hand. Although he looked like a cowboy, she would bet he had never done any manual labor in his life.

"I remember you, too, Ellen." He dropped her hand quickly after the handshake. "Are you sure you must run off? I can see I make you a bit nervous and I don't blame you. Here I am trying to pick you up in the middle of a dangerous city. I guess you're right to be careful, but I was hoping, since this is our second meeting . . ." His smile was charming.

Suddenly Ellen heard Maggie's voice in her head. "He's not asking you to come to his apartment. It's a public restaurant. What harm could it do?"

"It could do a lot of harm," Ellen answered.

Jim's face fell. "I understand. I had hoped I looked harmless. I am, you know. Divorced, unattached, employed, charming." He paused. "Lonely." His look managed to combine Don Juan and Lassie.

In spite of herself, Ellen started to laugh. "I guess I'm just being overly cautious. I'm sorry. You really are being quite nice." Ellen heard Maggie's applause, then the sound faded.

"Hooray," Jim said. "Does that mean you'll let me buy you dinner? I can explain all the nuances of the menu. Have you ever had Indian food before?"

"No." Ellen was again completely flustered. "I mean, no, I've never had Indian food before but yes, I'd love to join you for dinner. And no, you can't buy me dinner but we can go dutch."

Smiling, Jim nodded. "Wonderful." He placed his hand in the small of Ellen's back and guided her down the few steps into the small dining area. The restaurant seated about three dozen, with soft beige linen tablecloths and candle-lamps on each table. Since it was still early, they had their choice of tables and Jim chose a well-lit table off to one side. Ellen was glad he hadn't chosen something dark and secluded.

When Ellen was seated, Jim said, "They don't have a liquor license so we'll have to settle for herb tea, if that's all right with you."

"Sure," Ellen said, interlacing her fingers in her lap so she'd have something to do with her hands. During the moment's silence that followed, Ellen's mind churned. What should she say? How should she act? Should she have let him pay for dinner? She reached for her water glass but her hands were shaking so hard that she was sure she'd spill something so she replaced her hands in her lap, fumbling with her napkin.

"Listen, Ellen," Jim said, "it doesn't take a genius to see that you're really nervous about this. You look like a cornered animal ready to bolt at the first wrong move. How can I help you to relax?"

"I'm relaxed," Ellen protested.

"Right. And you always shred your napkin in Indian restaurants."

Ellen looked down and saw that the paper in her lap was torn into several long strips. She had the good grace to smile, weakly. "I'm sorry. This isn't the real me, I guess. I'm not much for dating."

"So what is the real you?"

"I'm a solitary person, quite used to eating alone. And I'm certainly not used to being picked up by strange men."

Jim raised an eyebrow the same way Maggie did. "I don't think I'm that strange."

Ellen laughed nervously. "I didn't mean that. Oh, damn. I'm a wreck. I have no clue what to say, how to act, what to do." At that moment, the waiter brought two cups of steaming tea.

After the brief reprieve, Jim said, "Why don't you do what you want, say what you think, and let's see what happens? You said that you don't date often."

"I don't date at all, really."

"I can't imagine why not. Are you new to the city?"

"I'm from upstate. I came into a little money and I decided to visit here." Surprisingly, she talked for several minutes, responding to Jim's gentle, non-intimate questions. "Now that you know the basics about me how about telling me a little about you," Ellen said, more interested than she cared to admit to herself.

"I'm thirty-eight and, as I told you before, divorced. No children. My ex didn't want any."

"And you did?"

"I didn't at first, but then over the two years Carrie and I were married, I realized that, to her, children meant permanence, something she didn't really want, and I did. Slowly it dawned on me that we were looking for totally different things so we split just over a year ago."

"Was it difficult?"

"Not nearly as difficult as I thought it was going to be, but I'm still not used to Saturdays. When you're married, you always have a date for Saturday night. When you're alone, the empty Saturdays become a symbol of something, so when I don't have other plans, I eat out." He hesitated, then continued, "To be honest I lied when I said I was planning on having dinner here. I hadn't decided where to eat so when I saw you heading across town I hoped you were alone. I'll admit I was looking for an excuse to talk to you again, so when you paused in front of The Flower of India, I said I was planning to eat here. I was anxious for company and hoped you were, too."

He was a nice man, neither a molester nor a millionaire. Just a lonely guy looking for company. Ellen suddenly realized that she was lonely, too, and was glad to have someone to share a little time with. Usually she was content with her own company, but now she found she was enjoying having someone to talk to. "Actually, the company's nice for a change." When the waiter arrived, he and Jim carefully explained many of the dishes on the menu. "I don't think I like spicy food," Ellen confessed.

"Most of the dishes here can be prepared anywhere from

mild to spicy," the waiter explained with a heavy Indian accent.

"Why don't we order the assorted appetizers and two main dishes? That way you can sample several different things. I'll get a few of my favorite condiments, too. Are you game?"

Am I game? she thought. "Sure. Why don't you pick two things you like and I'll sample everything?"

Jim ordered several items and the conversation flowed easily until the plate of appetizers arrived. The waiter placed it in the center of the table, then carefully wiped two small plates and placed one in front of each of them. Jim pointed to a chunk of bright-red meat. "This is tandoori chicken, an Indian specialty. A tandoor is a clay oven that bakes whatever you put inside, usually chicken, lamb, or shrimp marinated in yogurt." He leaned forward and whispered, conspiratorially, "It's frequently very dry because the chicken is cooked without the skin. It's one of my least favorite meats but in small bits it's not too bad."

Ellen grinned as he described the other things in the assortment. She tried the tandoori and had to agree with Jim, tasty, but very dry. The ground meat was delicious and the vegetable-filled pastry was unusual and wonderful.

When she grinned, Jim said, "I'm glad you're pleased," and the friendly atmosphere continued as the main course arrived. He showed her how to use her *chapati,* an Indian flat bread, to pick up delicately spiced pieces of lamb in a creamy sauce, flavored with crushed almonds.

"I'm amazed," Ellen said as she licked her fingers. "This is delicious and not spicy at all."

"Would you like to taste this one?" he asked, indicating a bowl filled with lumps of meat covered with a thick green-brown sauce. "It's a bit more . . . interesting." He spooned a small piece of meat and a bit of sauce onto her bread. "It's called *murgh saag*. It's chicken with a spinach sauce. I'll warn you, it's got a small kick so start with a small bite. If you don't like it, give it to me. It's one of my favorites."

Ellen tasted. "It's great. I've never tasted anything like this before, and I'm sorry I haven't."

"Not giving it to me?"

"Not a chance." Later, when she reached for her water glass, he intercepted her hand. "If your mouth's a little hot, take a bit of the *raita*. It's yogurt with cucumber and spices. It will cool your mouth much more quickly than water." When she smiled at the cooling effect of the raita Jim grinned. "That's my girl." Then he blushed. "I didn't mean that the way it came out. Of course you're not my girl."

"I know that," Ellen said, helping herself to some rice sprinkled with carrots and peas, and covering it with a bit of the spinach sauce. Sensing his sudden discomfort, she added, "Now it's time for you to relax. I hope we've passed the really awkward part." She handed him the lamb plate. "Have some more."

The rest of the meal passed with comfortable conversation. She learned that he was a computer programmer and worked for a company that made plumbing supplies, maintaining its Web site and order-entry system. He had been born and raised in Texas, and for the past fifteen years had lived in Manhattan several blocks south of her apartment.

After a dessert of something called *gulaab jamun,* a spherical pastry swimming in a honey sauce, they sipped tea and waited for the check. Jim made no protest when she handed him money to cover her half. Finally, they walked outside. "Can I walk you home?" he asked.

"It's a little soon for you to know where I live."

"That's fine, as long as you don't disappear. May I have your phone number at least, so maybe we can do this again some time?"

Ellen sensed that he was trying to sound casual but that this was important to him. If she were to admit it, it was important to her as well. "Sure." She wrote the number on a small piece of paper and handed it to him. "Thanks for a delightful evening. I'm sorry I'm so difficult, but I hope you'll forgive me."

"I certainly do. Someone from a small town like you are should be cautious. There are a lot of kooks and weirdos out here." He pulled a card out of his wallet. "Here's my name, address, phone number, e-mail address, pager number, and all that. Is it okay if I call you in a week or so?"

"I'll look forward to that." As Ellen watched Jim walk to the corner and turn south on Second Avenue, she realized that she was looking forward to seeing him again.

When she arrived in her apartment, she was grinning. She had had a dinner date with a man—and it felt wonderful. She undressed and, as she was about to flip on the TV she spied the CD player on her bedside table. She was in just the right mood for a story, ready to have her horizons widened. She stretched out on the bed, turned down the light, and pressed play.

CHAPTER 7

The narrator's voice was sexy, the background music soft and sensual. Ellen found that her body tingled all over. This story began the same way as all the others.

"Is there magic in the world? Skeptics doubt that magic exists, or ever did exist. Are they right? I don't know, but there are still a few people who are willing to keep an open mind, people who believe in old stories, ancient legends, and possibilities. Like the possibilities inherent in the Ring of Obedience.

"'Would you like your lover to obey your every wish, lady?' the old man asked.

"'Sure, who wouldn't,' MJ said, amused at the off-the-wall question the ancient peddler asked. Disregarding his salesman-like approach, she walked to the other

side of his street-corner display of watches and rings and looked down at the usual clutter of knock-off watches.

" 'I have just the thing for you,' the man said.

" 'Actually I'm looking for a birthday gift for my husband.' She shook her head at the knock-off watches—Omaga and Rollflex—then moved around to the group of rings. She picked up a silver wolf's head, then peered at a skull. No. Not right. He wasn't the skull type. She realized the old man was watching her so she picked up a large gold-looking signet ring with a gothic S on it. 'No. I don't think there's anything here he'd like.' She put the signet ring back on the tray and turned to leave, disappointed. Her husband, Steve's birthday dinner was that night and she still hadn't found anything to give him.

" 'But what would you like?' the vendor asked. MJ glanced back at him, then looked a bit longer. He was much older than the usual run-of-the-mill sidewalk vendor, with piercing deep blue eyes that seemed to see to her soul. He looked both spooky and wise although how those two things could go together she had no idea.

" 'What I want isn't the question. It's not my birthday, it's his.'

" 'You said you would like your husband to obey your every wish.' The man picked up a Celtic knot ring of woven strands of gold and silver. 'This will do that for you.'

"MJ took the ring from the vendor's hand. As he blathered on about obedience, she tuned him out. The ring really would be perfect for Steve, she thought. He loved unusual things and he was of ancient Irish heritage. It looked like it would be the right size, too. 'How much?'

" 'It's priceless.'

"Yeah, right, *she thought.* Here goes the part I hate. Bargaining. *'I'm sure it is, but how much?'*

" 'He who wears it must obey she who gave it. You'll see.'

"Enough. Then, as MJ started to put the ring down the man said, 'Fifty dollars.'

" 'You've got to be kidding! Fifty dollars for something from a pushcart? Not a chance.'

" 'You have no idea what you're passing up,' he said. 'This could mean everything to you. I can let you have the Ring of Obedience for forty dollars, but that's my final offer. Pass it up at your own peril.'

"MJ was about to replace the ring on the vendor's tray when she made a rash decision. It would probably turn Steve's finger green but what the hell. It was really right for him, and the old guy seemed so sincere. 'Ring of Obedience. Forty dollars. Okay, I'll take it.'

" 'Good. Very good.' As MJ rummaged through her purse for her wallet, the man continued, 'Just place it on his finger and from then on he won't be able to resist any suggestion you give him. And he won't be able to remove the ring himself. The only way to get it off is for you to take it from his hand. Of course it will only work on the man you love, not anyone else. Do you understand?'

"No reason not to humor the guy. 'Right. Obedience. Only I can take it off his finger. Got it.' She handed him two twenties and he gave her a small blue velvet box for the ring.

" 'If he puts it on your finger, you'll be under the same power. You will be unable to resist anything he wants you to do.'

" 'Sure. Anything you say.' She tucked the ring into the box and slipped it into her pocketbook.

"That evening, she and Steve went to a fancy Italian restaurant to celebrate his twenty-eighth birthday. After a glass of wine, she pulled the small velvet box from her purse and placed it on the table between them. 'Happy birthday, sweetheart.'

"He picked up the box, opened it, and stared. 'Wow. This is fantastic.' He pulled the ring out and gazed at it beneath the light from the small candle on the table. 'It's really great. Wherever did you find it?'

" 'I hate to admit it, but I got it on a street corner. It will probably turn your finger all kinds of colors but I really liked it and thought it would look fabulous on you.'

"When Steve started to put the ring on, MJ took it from him. 'Let me.' She slipped it onto his right ring finger, where it fit perfectly.

" 'Oh, baby,' Steve said, leaning forward. 'It looks just wonderful.'

"MJ leaned toward him and they kissed softly. At that moment the waiter arrived. 'May I take your order?'

" 'MJ?'

" 'Why don't you order for me?' she said.

" 'Certainly.' Without hesitation, Steve ordered veal with pasta and salads for both of them.

" 'Very good, sir,' the waiter said, striding toward the kitchen.

"During dinner Steve kept admiring the ring. 'You know, maybe it would look better on my other hand.' He pulled at the ring, but it wouldn't come off. 'Hmm. It seems to be stuck. Never mind. It looks great right there.'

"MJ reached for his hand and easily slipped the ring off. 'That was easy. Are you sure it was stuck?'

" 'It was stuck fast.' Steve slipped the ring onto the index finger of his left hand. 'I wonder how you got it off so easily.' He looked at his hand, then shook his head. 'Nah. It looked better on my right hand.' Again he struggled and again the ring wouldn't budge.

"MJ remembered the peddler's words. 'He won't be able to remove the ring himself. The only way to get it off is for you to take it from his hand.' She reached over and easily slipped the ring from his left hand and re-placed it on his right. 'Hmm.'

" 'It's really funny the way it seems to get stuck when I try to get it off yet you have no trouble.'

" 'Yeah. It is curious, isn't it.'

"Throughout the meal, MJ thought about the ring. A couple of times she asked Steve to do something really simple and each time he did it without question. Just coincidence, she thought. Should I give it a test? A real one? Nah. I can't really believe what some vendor says. 'Baby, how about going dancing after dinner.' Steve hated dancing and always refused.

" 'Sure. Sounds like a great idea.'

"MJ's eyes widened. Could this be? 'But it's your birthday. Shouldn't we do something you want to do?'

" 'If you want to go dancing, then dancing it shall be.'

"Did she really want to go dancing if this ring thing truly worked? Not a chance. She wanted to be home, in bed. However, the ring needed a more serious test. 'Actually, I'd like you to go into the men's room and take off your jockey shorts, then come back and hand them to me.'

"Shit, here it comes, she thought. He'll burst out

laughing and that will be that. *She was grinning, ready to enjoy a shared joke, when Steve stood up and, without a word, headed toward the men's room. Moments later he returned, handed her his shorts and sat back down as though it was the most normal thing in the world.*

"This is too weird, but too funky not to take advantage of. 'You know how I love your cock,' MJ said, 'so I want to know it's ready for me for later. Are you hot?'

" 'You know I am always hot for you.'

" 'Is it hard?'

"Steve grinned sheepishly. 'Yes. Actually the feeling of my dick rubbing against the inside of my zipper is making me really horny.'

" 'Then unzip. I want to see.'

"Steve looked puzzled, but reached into his lap and, from what MJ could see from her side of the table, unzipped his pants. 'This is really kinky,' Steve said, 'but I seem to want to do whatever you want. Silly, isn't it?'

" 'Yes,' MJ said, 'it really is.' She slipped off her shoe and placed her stocking-covered foot in Steve's lap. Sure enough, his cock was naked, poking from the opening in the front of his pants. Naked and hard as a rock. She rubbed her foot up and down the length of him, smiling as she saw how distracted he was. 'Think about my foot,' she purred. 'Think of how good it feels, how hot you're getting, how difficult it is not to come.'

" 'Shit, baby, why are you torturing me?'

" 'Is it really such torture?'

"Steve grinned. 'Yes. Well, no. Your foot feels wonderful.'

" 'Good. Then concentrate on it.' There was utter silence at the table as MJ stroked Steve's hard cock with her stocking-clad foot. Finally she said, 'What you really *want to do is to rub your cock until you come, isn't it? Right here in this restaurant.'*

" 'Yes,' Steve groaned.

" *'I would never embarrass you, of course, so you can cover your hand and cock with your napkin. Then rub yourself until you come. I'll just keep stroking you with my foot since that feels so sexy.'*

"Steve looked at MJ. *'It feels decadent and kinky, but I really want to do it.'* As she watched, he covered his lap with his napkin and rubbed his cock. The bemused look on his face was quickly replaced with one of rapture. Suddenly MJ could feel the spasms rock his erection and the wet stickiness on her foot. He had really done it. This was truly amazing.

"When he had cleaned himself up and they were having coffee, MJ confessed and told Steve all about the peddler and his story about the ring. *'I didn't believe it,'* she said, *'but it seemed to work. You appeared to be incapable of resisting whatever I said.'*

" *'Could it be?'*

" *'I certainly didn't think so,'* she said, *'but consider what just happened. You masturbated right here in public. Would you ever have done anything like that before tonight?'*

"Steve shook his head. *'No. I guess not. That's some kind of power. You could really use it for evil.'*

" *'The old man swore that it would only work between us and I'd never do anything that I didn't know you'd like.'* She slowly pulled the ring from his finger. *'I'll only use it when we agree that you should put it on. It does have great erotic potential, doesn't it?'*

" *'Phew. It certainly does.'* Steve took the ring and gazed at MJ. *'What happens if I put it on your finger?'*

" *'I obey you.'*

"Steve motioned to the waiter. 'Check please.' He turned to MJ. 'Let's go home. We've got to play with this thing some more.' "

Ellen took a deep breath. Her entire body had reacted to the heat in the story. *Could I ever do something like that?* she wondered. She thought about the dinner that she had shared with Jim and pictured herself in MJ's place and Jim in Steve's. Jim had his hand in his crotch, so hot and under her control that he masturbated in public. As she thought about it, her hand rubbed her mound and slid back to her clit. Her orgasm was almost too quick, crashing over her suddenly and completely.

The following day was warm and sunny so, rising quite late in the morning, she dressed in a new outfit, a vibrant green silk shirt and a pair of tailored beige slacks. She added a long, thin brown belt, slender gold earrings, and her leather vest and headed to the local diner where she often stopped for breakfast. As she walked along Fifty-second Street she saw a small restaurant advertising a champagne brunch. *Why not?* she thought. Something different.

After a leisurely meal with two glasses of orange juice and champagne, she again wandered around the city. About three, as she walked back uptown she spied a small antique clock in the window of a dusty antique store. Inside she asked the clerk the price and was flabbergasted to find out that it was more than three hundred dollars. "Sorry," she said. As she headed for the door, the woman called, "Wait. Maybe I could do something for you." She went into a back room and returned with an index card. With an exaggerated sigh, she said, "I could let it go for two seventy-five."

"Two and a quarter and not a cent more," Ellen said, wondering where the words had come from. She thought the clock was beautiful and would look just perfect in her living room but to spend that much money frivolously was silly. She hated bargaining, but still . . .

"I'm so sorry. I couldn't let it go for anything less than two fifty."

Two hundred and fifty dollars. This was ridiculous. "Okay," she heard herself say. "I'll take it."

"You've made a good decision," the woman said and took the clock and Ellen's credit card to the rear of the store. Soon Ellen was walking toward her apartment with the clock in a shopping bag. Her apartment. She was beginning to think of it that way. She stopped at the corner and added a large bunch of flowers to her purchase. *My apartment.*

The next day was Monday, the day of the art class. She considered not going, but no. The butterfly was going to venture out of her cocoon, and without Maggie's help, even if it killed her. She looked over her new purchases, but finally dressed in an old pair of jeans and a sweatshirt and added her navy windbreaker. Painting clothes, not a stylish outfit. She wasn't here to impress anyone, just learn to paint and she certainly wasn't trying to impress Kevin. One man in her life at a time was enough. So, with her art-supply box in hand, she headed for The Templeton Gallery.

She entered the gallery and followed the signs to the second-floor workshop where the classes were held. The room was almost the size of the entire gallery, with windows on two sides and several skylights. The air smelled of art, of oil and turpentine, thinner, and fixative. She saw Kevin standing at the side of the room, looking over the shoulder of a middle-aged man who held a charcoal pencil in his hand. As she looked around, Ellen saw that there were a total of six people, each standing in front of an easel with paper clipped to backing, working silently with charcoal, trying to get the right perspective on a vase of flowers on a pedestal table at the front of the room. Canvases covered

with cloths were propped against the walls around the pe-
rimeter of the room. Shelves held what Ellen imagined were
sculptures, also covered. Several pieces of furniture were
scattered around the periphery.

She stood in the doorway for a moment until Kevin spotted her and rushed over. "It's Ellen, isn't it?" He was dressed
in casual gray jeans and a soft blue V-neck sweater that
brought out the blue of his eyes and showed a large amount
of heavy black chest hair. He had pushed the sweater's
sleeves up to reveal strong forearms covered with more thick,
black hair. "You've changed your hair."

Flattered that he remembered her name, and flabbergasted
that he had noticed her new look, Ellen nodded weakly. "I-
I-I thought I'd try out a class and see what I can do."

"We're delighted to have you. I'd introduce you around
but right now everyone is doing a five-minute exercise." He
guided her to an empty easel and helped her set up a pad of
textured paper. "We're playing with line today, trying to get
the essence of a shape with as few lines as possible." He
found a charcoal pencil in her box and helped her sharpen
it. "Just relax and try to get with the flow of what's going
on. I'll come back to you later." At that moment a timer that
had been ticking away in the background sounded. "Okay,
everyone." He put a book and a candle in a brass holder on
the small table, cranked the timer and said, "Next. Go!"

Ellen took her charcoal pencil and quickly sketched the
items in front of her. In what seemed only seconds, the timer
sounded again. "Okay," Kevin said, as he added a bowl of
fruit and a few soft brushes to the book and candle. "Here's
another. Take fifteen minutes with this one and I'll come
around and see how everyone's doing." He repositioned the
cloth on which the items rested then said, "Okay. Go!"

As Ellen worked she noticed that Kevin wandered from
easel to easel, commenting, adjusting, suggesting, all in a

gentle and supportive tone. When he arrived behind her he said, "As you finish an exercise, take a new sheet and put the previous one beside you so I can look at your work without disturbing you."

Ellen flipped back a page and tore off the previous exercise. Kevin held it up and studied it as Ellen looked with him. Each object was portrayed in only a few lines, but the overall effect was not only shape but solidity. "This is quite good for a rank amateur. You've got a good hand and a good eye. It's quite obvious, however, that you've had no formal training." He looked from her work to her. "I'm sorry. That came out sounding insulting and I didn't mean it that way."

"You're right, though. I've never had a lesson. I just draw what I like, and it seems to come out okay."

Ellen saw genuine appreciation in his eyes. "It most certainly does. Your sense of line is really wonderful."

"I haven't drawn anything in more years than I care to think about. Do you think I can make something that will give me pleasure?"

"That's an interesting way to put it. Most people are concerned with whether they can create something salable."

"I'm not interested in selling my work, just enjoying it." Ellen realized that this was the first time she had ever done something for pure pleasure, without an ulterior motive.

"I always rant and rave about people who are only interested in the monetary aspect of art. In my mind, if you get joy out of what you're creating, that's the object of the game. If you sell something, so much better." He glanced at the timer at the front of the room. "This arrangement has only another minute, but we'll do several more. The class lasts until twelve. Stay after and let's talk." When Ellen nodded, Kevin hustled to the front of the room. "Okay," he said, "let's do another fifteen-minute exercise."

Two hours later only Kevin and Ellen remained in the workroom. Toward the end of class, Kevin had introduced Ellen to the other students. Each was warm and open with, "Glad to meet yous," and "Welcomes." One woman suggested that one day they have lunch after class. "What a nice group you have," she said when Kevin had finished cleaning up the front of the room.

"I seem to attract the nicest and most talented people." He stood behind her and Ellen could feel the warmth of his breath on her neck as he talked. "You included, of course, but I do have a collection of very talented artists in my classes. You met Joseph Overman, the guy with the heavy eyebrows and the glasses." Ellen pictured the inept-looking man who seemed to have trouble seeing the end of his brush through his amazingly thick glasses. "He's having a one-man show at The Morris next month."

"He is? What's The Morris?"

"A very prestigious gallery in Soho. It's quite an honor for him."

"And for you, too, I'd say."

Kevin nodded, then lapsed into silence gazing at her work, finally saying, "You know, you've really got talent. I hope you'll continue to come here."

She had no idea whether she actually had talent or whether Kevin was just saying that to get her to sign up for a series of classes, but she found she didn't care. She was doing something just for the hell of it, and she hadn't had as much fun in a long time. "I have no clue whether I have talent or not, but I really enjoyed this morning. I think I'd like to come back. I've read your brochure and I think I can deal with the cost of ten lessons to start."

"Wonderful." He took her credit card and hustled downstairs, returning several minutes later with a receipt for her to sign and a handful of signed business cards. "You turn in one of these each lesson. That way I don't have to keep track of what days you come. I do classes Mondays, Wednesdays, and Fridays, and my brother, Sean, does them on Tuesdays and Thursdays. He sculpts so unless you want to play with clay, come on my days. Most classes, like this morning's, are applicable to any medium, but I have some special ones from time to time that focus on techniques for a specific medium. There will always be a schedule posted both up here and downstairs. Why watercolors, by the way?"

"I used to paint when I was a kid and I always enjoyed poster paint so I guess I just thought that made sense. Otherwise, I've no fixed ideas."

Kevin tipped his head to one side. "Let me ask you this. If you could paint anything in the world: landscapes, portraits, still lifes, animals, what would you paint?" When Ellen didn't answer immediately, he continued, "Close your eyes and see yourself in your living room, gazing up at a blank wall. Now see a frame there, filled with something you created. You're happy to look at it, pleased that it came out so well. Got that?"

"Yes," Ellen said, eyes closed.

"Okay. What's in the frame?"

"It's a landscape, I guess. Soft green trees and a lake."

From close behind her, Kevin whispered, "Tell me more."

"There are flowers and puffy white clouds. Two people are having a picnic. They are obviously laughing and enjoying the warm sun but they are small and you can't make out their faces."

"Okay," he said softly. "That's a good place to start. Just because you're thinking about landscapes doesn't mean you can overlook the basics though. It doesn't free you from work and exercises like the ones we were doing today. You need to master line and form, shape and contour. You must learn about composition and texture." He grasped her

shoulders and stood close to her back. "And in your painting, were those people you and me by any chance?"

Startled, Ellen realized that she hadn't had any sexual
thoughts about Kevin since she arrived, but now her mind
was filled with the feel and smell of him. The hair on the
back of her neck prickled from the feel of his breath. "You
know, of course, that I paint. I was wondering. Would you
pose for me some afternoon?"

"Me?" Ellen thought about her fantasy. Being alone with
Kevin, just the two of them. *Be real, Ellen,* she told herself.
He's just a painter looking for a free model.

"Sure," she said, trying to keep her voice light. "Why
not?" Don't get carried away, she lectured herself.

"Good. That's great. Could you sit for me one afternoon
this week? I'm just finishing something, but Thursday would
be wonderful."

"Can you just take time from the gallery like that?"

"My brother Sean and I co-own the Templeton. He sculpts
while I cover the downstairs, then I paint while he gallery-
sits. Could you come on Thursday?"

Why the hell not? "Okay."

"I need to tell you something that might change your
mind." She could feel Kevin's sigh. "I was considering letting
you show up then telling you but I have too much respect
for you to create an awkward scene. I paint nudes."

Ellen felt the heat scorch her cheeks. "Nudes? Why me?"
she squeaked, unable to get anything else sensible out of her
mouth.

Kevin took her shoulders and turned her around to face
him. "Honestly? You have a wonderful combination of sensuality and reticence, power and modesty, curiosity and hes-
itancy. If I could portray that, I'd be a genius. I want to try."
He brushed her lower lip with his thumb. "And you have
such a sexy mouth."

Ellen couldn't get any coherent thoughts through her brain. It was as though her entire body was paralyzed and all the energy of movement flowed into her swirling thoughts.

Kevin cleared his throat. "I'm sorry. I've embarrassed you and I didn't intend it at all. Really. I'm not making a pass at you, I was just being truthful, something that often gets me into trouble. Please. Feel free to say no, but also consider saying yes. The human body is so beautiful that it's what I enjoy painting most."

Ellen realized that her hands had crept up until they were covering her breasts. She certainly didn't have a body that men wanted to paint.

"Let me show you a few of my paintings and maybe you'll understand." She didn't protest when he led her into a small side room. Paintings stood on the floor, balanced against the walls. They were all of nudes, reclining, seated, standing, posed and in natural positions.

"These are very good," Ellen said, overwhelmed by the quality of the work. "They live. They almost breathe."

Kevin's smile lit his face. "That's what I hope people will see in them."

"The women are all so lovely," Ellen said, more sure than ever that she couldn't pose for him.

"Are they? Look more closely. They are all just ordinary women."

Ellen took a better look and quickly realized that Kevin was right. There were no perfect bodies, no models' shapes yet all the women were, each in her own way, beautiful. "Why do they all look beautiful?"

"Because, when I paint them, they feel beautiful. That's all it really takes to make a woman beautiful."

"Not really," she said, but she continued to stare at the room full of nude women.

"Really. Let me prove it to you. Let me sketch you on Thursday. Come at about two. If you don't want to stay, I'll understand. If you just want to sit, fully clothed, and let me try to capture that wonderful attitude, that will be enough for me."

She could keep her clothes on, yet he could make her look beautiful? Should she do it?

"Listen, Ellen. I'll be here at two, waiting, hoping you'll show up. If you do, we will do only what makes you comfortable. If you're not comfortable I can't paint you anyway. Please come. But if you don't, I'll understand, and of course you'll still come to my classes. Okay?"

"I'll think about it."

"Bravo!" Lucy screamed. "She's going to go for it."

"Lucy, you promised not to eavesdrop," Angela snapped.

"I know, but she's such a fascinating case. You know me. I can resist anything but temptation."

"Luce, you're incorrigible. Don't promises mean anything to you? How's she ever going to feel like she has any privacy?"

"She doesn't."

"I know that, but she doesn't."

Large letters streamed across Lucy's computer screen. "LUCY—YOU AREN'T GETTING ANY WORK DONE. PAY ATTENTION TO BUSINESS AND STAY OUT OF THINGS THAT DON'T CONCERN YOU."

"Yes, sir," Lucy said, returning to a stack of computer printouts. "But I decide what concerns me," she whispered.

CHAPTER 8

When Ellen wandered into the kitchen the following morning, Maggie was sitting waiting for her, a gift-wrapped box on the table in front of her. "I took the liberty of starting coffee," she said. She pushed the box toward Ellen as she settled across the table. "This is for you."

Ellen settled at the tiny table and picked up the flat box, wrapped in shiny red paper with a black ribbon and intricately tied bow. "You didn't have to get me anything. You've been so much help already."

"It's not from me. I found it in the changing room."

"Changing room?"

"The changing room is where I am just before you see me. I'm just there, and there are clothes waiting for me appropriate for what I will do that day. I dress, then open the door and I'm here, or wherever. Lord the verbiage is so difficult." She combed her fingers through her hair. "Anyway, I found this on a bench and the card's addressed to you."

Ellen took the package and pulled off the attached card. The envelope was small and black as was the business card inside. "For Thursday," it said in white ink. "Knock him dead. Love, Lucy."

"It's from Lucy," Ellen said, barely able to keep her jaw from dropping. She pulled the paper off the box and opened it. In a nest of black tissue paper lay a tiny lacy bra and matching bikini panties, both in a soft blue. As Ellen held them up she realized that, while they were totally decent, they were also decadent, with carefully selected areas of thick and thin lace. "She's got to be kidding," Ellen said, gaping at the lingerie. "I couldn't wear anything like this."

"Why not, and what's happening on Thursday? And what day is it now?"

"Actually, it's Tuesday, and quite a bit has happened since I saw you last." She told Maggie all about Jim and dinner the previous Saturday evening. Then she spent several minutes discussing Kevin's painting class. "Oh, and he asked me to pose for him next Thursday." She ducked her head. "Nude."

"Wow. Quite a step out of your safe little cocoon, I'd say."

Ellen's head snapped up abruptly. "Just a damn minute. How does Lucy know about Thursday?" she snapped. "Has she been watching me again? I thought they both promised to stay out of my life."

Maggie held her hands up, palms outward. "Hold it. I have no control over Lucy. To be honest, I doubt that anyone has, except maybe her boss." She chuckled. "And I'm not even sure about him."

"The nerve of her." Ellen almost ran into the living room and dropped onto the sofa. She jumped up again and paced. "The nerve."

Maggie followed her into the living room, a coffee mug in

each hand. "I would suggest that you just don't think about her," she said with infuriating calm. "She's become more and more of a busybody lately, but she can't really affect what you do unless you let her." She handed Ellen her coffee and settled in an overstuffed chair. Changing the subject she asked, "What are you going to do about Thursday? I hope you're going to pose for him."

"I don't know," Ellen said with a long sigh, propping her feet on the coffee table. "Part of me wants to be brave and daring, to go along with my new look and all, but part of me is terrified that I'll get myself into something that I can't get out of."

"I know you don't know Kevin very well but from the feelings that you get, do you think you have to worry about him attacking you? Do you think he'd stop if you said no to something?"

Ellen thought a moment. "I think he would. I don't know why I say that. He might be a total con artist, bilking unsuspecting women out of their life savings for art lessons and midday sex." When Maggie raised her usual skeptical eyebrow, Ellen said, "Okay. He's probably not on *America's Most Wanted* and somehow I do trust him."

"So what you're saying is that it's *you* that you don't trust."

Ellen took a long time going into the kitchen and refilling her coffee cup. Maggie was right, of course. What she didn't trust were her own feelings and needs. Until recently she hadn't realized how much she had been missing in life. Sure, she had been depressed when Gerry moved to the city, but she had made a life for herself without a man in it. But was that really life? Didn't she need more? Wasn't that why, deep down beyond the obvious, she had come to the city? Ellen had never been particularly introspective but now, as she finally looked into herself, she had to admit that she was curious about men and sex and relationships. More and more, thoughts about what she'd been missing had been filtering into her consciousness.

As she returned with her coffee, Ellen picked up the conversation. "I guess what I'm scared to death of is being out of my league, of discovering that I know nothing about loving." Tears started to gather in her eyes. "I'm terrified of having someone like Kevin make a pass at me, then being so inept that he laughs at me or just gives up in frustration."

"No one's born knowing or confident," Maggie said, handing Ellen a tissue from the pocket of her jeans. "Every woman in the world has had doubts like yours from time to time. Women who've been out of the dating scene for a while wonder whether anyone will ever be interested in them again. Some women stay with men who are incredibly bad for them because they are frightened that they will never have sex again."

"You never had doubts," Ellen said with a sniff.

"Of course I did. Not as much in my later years, of course, although I was often worried that a new man would be disappointed in my body or my performance. In my early years, I was nervous almost all the time, but it's attitude that matters. If you force yourself to feel confident, then the confidence will become real very quickly. It's like 'Whistle a Happy Tune.' Make believe you're brave and all."

Ellen smiled through her tears. "I can't imagine you've ever being scared of a man and his opinion of you."

"I remember when my friend Frank's boss, Norman, called me the first time. We talked for almost an hour. I knew it was an interview of sorts, on Frank's recommendation. He was judging me, not on my sexual prowess but on my charm and intelligence. He must have found me pleasant enough because he invited me join him, his wife and a nameless, important bigwig from out of town at a political fund-raiser the following Saturday evening. I was going to entertain the client in whatever way presented itself. He didn't want me to tell the client that I was being paid and I wasn't totally comfortable with that, but at that moment I would have agreed to anything."

"A phone interview for a job as a prostitute?"

"Sounds a bit strange, but it actually made sense. He wanted to know whether I could make intelligent conversation and be entertaining outside of the bedroom. Finally he told me about the dinner. The candidate was an archconservative and I was a flaming liberal but somehow I agreed to attend anyway. And, of course, the money was a great incentive. Norman suggested some cover story and that was that.

"As the evening of the dinner approached I almost backed out. What did I know about which fork to use or how to make small talk with some guy who would know that I was a paid companion? What would he expect? Would I be able to make love with someone just for money? I was a wreck."

"I look at you and I can't imagine you not confident. How long ago was that?" Ellen asked, her attention riveted on Maggie's story.

"More years than I care to think about. I began in the business in 1974 or thereabouts."

"How did it all start, if you'll pardon me for asking?"

Maggie sipped her coffee. "I had been married. It was great sex but nothing else. After a few years, we split and I spent months lonely and horny as hell. I was in my early thirties, at my sexual peak with lots of energy and nowhere to spend it. One evening, on my way home from work, I stopped for a drink and a really nice guy picked me up. To make a long story short, Frank and I ended up in bed together, sharing a very satisfying night, and lots more after that. When he understood where I was in my life, he suggested that, if I loved sex, I should get paid for it. He mentioned me to his boss who often had to find companions for lonely businessmen. That was Norman."

"Didn't Frank mind sharing you?"

"He wasn't interested in a permanent relationship and had a very open mind. He liked it that I was happy and he knew I needed the money."

"Wow. You found a real gem right off the bat."

"He was pretty terrific, but about a year after I met him he got transferred to the West Coast and out of my life."

"You didn't go with him?"

"Sweetie, I told you. It wasn't that kind of relationship. Understand this. These men—Frank was the first of many— were fun to be with, date, and fuck, but not long-term material for either of us. I had long before decided that I wasn't a one-man woman, and I made that perfectly clear to all the men I dated more than once. I like variety, experimentation, originality. I like the thrill of a new bedroom with a new partner."

"Didn't any of the men get serious?"

"Oh, sure. There was one man, Paul, who kept proposing. I knew he wasn't really serious. We were great in bed and had lots in common but it just wasn't enough. And, of course, he was years younger than I was."

Ellen sipped her coffee. "I want someone who's interested in building a life together with me."

"Great. Go for that, but you have to kiss a lot of frogs to find one handsome prince, so if you learn to love kissing, it's all wonderful."

Laughing, Ellen almost choked on her coffee. "Boy, I've dated a few frogs in my time but not recently. Maybe that's why I want some permanence."

"What's right for me isn't necessarily right for you. If you want to find the right guy, however, you have to be brave and do some dating."

"Kevin's not a date. He's someone who wants me to pose nude. This could be sex, but it's not dating."

"Even if Kevin's not long-term material, he's experience. You know, it's easy to tell a frog from a prince, but it's much more difficult to tell Mr. Right from Mr. Almost-Right. You need to sample what's out there before you'll have any idea who's going to fit with you for the long haul."

"Brave. Right." Her sigh was loud. "Anyway, let's get back to you. You were telling me about your political dinner. Frank's boss Norman."

"Right. I decided that if I was going to be successful in the business, I had to look the part so I made myself over with hair, makeup, and nails, just as you did." She fluffed her short, curly hair. "Remember women were still going to bed in curlers so I found a cut that would still look good after a night's tumble. I spent almost a week's salary on a dress. It was black silk, bias cut, long and slender with classic lines that came straight across above my breasts with little, skinny straps. I reasoned that it wouldn't go out of style too quickly and would accessorize easily to change its look. I added a floral-print sequined jacket, black strappy sandals, and a plain gold necklace and earrings."

"Sounds gorgeous."

"You know, that dress really helped my confidence and I needed it that night. It almost became a fiasco." Maggie's thoughts drifted back to that evening.

"As planned, I arrived as the cocktail hour was ending and found a seating card with my name on it. I wended my way through crowds of black-tie–clad men and women in out-rageous gowns and found my table toward the front of the room. As I approached I recognized Norman from his description of himself over the phone. To make everyone feel at ease I was to pretend that I knew him and that he had invited me to fill the final empty seat at the table, which was to be next to my date. I transferred my small black beaded handbag to my left hand and extended my right. 'Norman,' I said. 'This is such a pleasure. I can't thank you enough for calling.'

" 'Maggie, darling,' Norman said, taking my hand and pulling my face close. 'It's been an age.' He bussed my cheek. 'What have you been doing with yourself?'

" 'Just this and that,' I said. 'You know how I hate talking about me. How have you been?'

"We made small talk for a few moments, then Norman introduced me around the table. 'And this is Walter O'Reilly from our Atlanta office,' he said, indicating an overweight man with an overly tight cummerbund that made him look like twenty pounds of mashed potatoes in a ten-pound sack. He had a real salesman smile, a florid complexion, and a roving eye. His gaze oscillated from my face to my cleavage.

" 'That's not Radar,' he said with a loud laugh. 'Just Walter.'

" 'Radar?' I asked, wondering whether I could go through with the evening.

" 'From *M*A*S*H*. Radar O'Reilly's real name is Walter. Don't you watch?'

" 'Of course,' I said, planting a smile on my face. 'Nice to meet you, not-Radar.' His laugh boomed so loudly that people at adjoining tables turned to look."

Ellen's nose wrinkled. "He sounds like quite a character."

"Oh, he was. I just stared, sure I was going to have to run for the hills. I thought about the money and shook his hand. *Confidence*, I told myself. *It's all in the attitude*."

"How did you deal with the fact that you were going to spend the night with someone who you didn't like?"

"I just went along minute to minute. I couldn't insult Norman or Walter so I just let myself drift, and made sure I looked like I was enjoying every second of everything." Maggie chuckled. "I had made my bed, so to speak, and now I had to lie in it.

"So Norman finished the introductions. 'This is Barrett Olkowski,' Norman said. 'He's a top chemist from our midwest research facility. He's worked on some of our most important breakthroughs and he's here for a symposium. He was going to spend the evening in his hotel room so I insisted that he get out for a few hours. I'm not sure, of course, that I did him any favors what with the boring speeches he'll be sitting through, but the food's usually good and, now that you're here, so's the company.'

"I pulled my gaze from not-Radar and considered Barrett. He was about my height, sort of owlish looking with soulful brown eyes and thinning hair. Norman guided me to a seat between Walter and Barrett."

"Were you supposed to be with Walter or Barrett?" Ellen asked.

"That's the silly part. As I sat down I realized that I didn't know which man was my date. Norman had neglected to tell me anything about the man I was being paid to entertain and he didn't pick up on my not-too-subtle hints. So I had to be nice to both of them, and in Walter's case, it wasn't easy. Barrett was a quiet guy, content to eat and let the conversation swirl around everyone else throughout the multi-course meal. Not-Radar, on the other hand, was boisterous, rude, and a general pain in the ass. He told nasty jokes, making fun of blacks, Jews, Polaks, as he called them, and anyone else he could get his mouth around. He also got his digs in on Liberals and Democrats."

"Didn't anyone complain?"

"Remember those were the days before political correctness when it was all right to tell jokes of any kind as long as someone laughed. I smiled and frequently cringed inwardly, crossing my fingers that Barrett was mine."

"How did you manage with the silverware and all?"

"I carefully watched what everyone else did and followed their lead. It really wasn't as difficult as I had feared. What was hard was making both men feel like they were special, while personally loathing not-Radar. I think that was the moment when I decided that I was never going to get into a situation like that again. I was going to chat with each client on the phone before any date. If I didn't like him, it was no dice. I wasn't ever going to do it just for the money again. That night, however, I was hooked. A deal's a deal and I was prepared to go ahead with whatever I had to."

"You really never did it just for the money again?"

"Never. I kept working for a while and I built up a nice little nest egg. As you've found out in the past few months, kiss-off money is the best thing there ever was."

"Kiss-off money?" Ellen asked.

"Money enough to tell anyone to kiss off, to quit your job, to tell any obnoxious slob, like not-Radar, that you're not available. You get the idea."

Ellen nodded as she considered her lottery winnings. She could tell Dr. Okamura to kiss off any time she wanted. It gave her a completely different outlook on life and, as Maggie said, it was, indeed, freeing. "Was not-Radar the guy you were supposed to be with, and how did it work out?"

"During the speeches Walter was on one side of me cheering on the candidate, a conservative who made Ronald Reagan look liberal while, on the other side of me, Barrett groaned from time to time. Finally the guy finished and many of the members of the audience got up to leave. In the confusion, I finally got to talk to Norman."

"So which guy was it?"

"Norman was horrified that he had neglected to tell me that important bit of information. 'I'm so sorry, Maggie,' he whispered. 'Walter showed up Friday afternoon and asked whether I had a ticket for tonight so I invited him along. Barrett's the guy I am paying you for. I didn't realize that I'd never told you the name of the man I wanted you to entertain. Barrett's such a shy guy but he's a cracker-jack chemist and a really nice man when you get to know him. He's single and, beneath it all, very lonely. I really just wanted to show him a good time in the big city. I didn't tell him about you and I'm hoping you can get him to unwind, in spite of himself. I want him to feel attractive, good about himself.'"

"I'll bet you were relieved," Ellen said.

"Yes, and no. I was delighted that Walter wasn't my date for the evening, but I wasn't sure I could deceive Barrett either."

"So what did you do?"

"As the place was emptying out, a dance band began to play some slow music. While Walter was talking to Norman, I asked Barrett to dance with me. I love slow-dancing and I was hoping to loosen him up a bit. While we danced I asked him about himself and got little more than one-syllable answers. A bit frustrated, I asked about his work and he told me it was all secret. Finally, as we were walking back to the table, he said, 'You don't have to be nice to me, you know.'

"I tried to look puzzled, although I knew exactly what he meant. 'I know I don't have to be nice to you.'

" 'Please,' he said, whirling to glare at me, 'I own a mirror. Let's be honest here. The only reason I can think of for your being nice to me is that you're a pro who Norman hired. He's threatened to do it for some time. I don't need a professional hooker to charm me into bed. I'm perfectly capable of taking care of myself.'

"I was flabbergasted that I had been that obvious, and a bit relieved that I wouldn't have to lie about it. 'I'm sure you are and I'm not going to deny that Norman invited me to be your date for the evening.' I wanted to find a way to just spend some time with him. He seemed like a scared rabbit and I found that I was becoming fond of him. 'Listen. You're right. I'm being paid for this, but if Norman doesn't see us spending time together, I don't get paid and, to be honest, I need the money. If we just sit for a while, or dance, later you can tell Norman you were really tired or something, so he wouldn't think that you didn't find me pleasant company.'"

"That was very clever. You're such a sweet person," Ellen said.

"I just like people, and I saw what Norman liked in Barrett. He was a really nice guy with an attitude problem a mile wide. His attitude problem totally eliminated mine. I convinced him to take pity on me so we sat at the table and just talked for a while. Later, as we danced, I could tell he was attracted to me. His palms got sweaty and he fumbled for his words when he held me. I rubbed my body against his and enjoyed the feeling of his excitement. 'You know I'm already paid for the evening,' I said, 'and I think we could be good together.' He looked dubious but I continued, 'Why don't we go up to your room and order a bottle of wine from room service? We don't have to do anything you don't want to but we can leave our options open.'"

"I could see uncertainty in his eyes. 'I'm not a charity case, you know.'"

"I cupped my hand over his erection. 'You don't need charity.' I took his hand, slipped it under my jacket and placed his palm over my breast. 'You may not know this but when a woman gets aroused, her nipples become erect.' I held his hand tightly. 'This isn't charity.'"

"I half-expected him to pull his hand back, but his eyes locked with mine. He said nothing, but he nodded." Maggie looked at Ellen. "Do you want to hear the details? I don't usually kiss and tell, but this was twenty-five years ago. I think the statute of limitations has run out."

"Sure," Ellen said, resting her elbows on the table. "I'm fascinated. How did you get around his shyness? That must be an unusual problem."

"It's funny but it's a more prevalent problem than I would have imagined. Men would call me, then chicken out. I'd arrive and they'd tell me that they'd changed their minds. Men have performance anxieties, too, and since I'm the pro they figure that if they can't get it up then they'll be humiliated."

"Really? I never considered that a man might be afraid like that."

"Me either. Anyway, Barrett and I had a conversation in the elevator. I decided to be completely honest and, by the way, I've been that way ever since." She drifted back to that evening and replayed the scene in her mind.

"Listen, Barrett, let me be completely straight with you. I'm really new at this entertainment business. I like you and I think you're a really nice guy and, frankly, you turn me on. I really like the shy type. I'm ever so glad that you know I'm a professional because I had already decided that I couldn't go on lying. I'd love to just sit and talk with you and, if something happens, that's fine. If not, fine, too. How about that?"

"You're a really nice lady," he said, "and, I must admit, you're sexy as hell. I've been thinking lewd thoughts about you all evening but I find that the idea that you're so—well—experienced, scares the shit out of me."

Maggie was delighted that Barrett had said more in one elevator ride than he had said all evening. She grabbed his

arm and pressed his elbow against the side of her breast.
"Let's just see where honesty gets us."

In his room Maggie removed her jacket while Barrett
called twenty-four-hour room service and ordered a bottle
of wine and two glasses. "Are you hungry?" he asked, holding his palm over the receiver.

Maggie's eyes lit up. "You know, I was so nervous about
the evening that I didn't eat much dinner. I'm starved."

"Burgers for two?" When Maggie eagerly nodded, Barrett
added two burger specials to his order. They chatted for a
while until the room-service waiter arrived and set up the
table for their midnight meal. Finally able to enjoy each
other's company, they gobbled their burgers.

Each plate had arrived with french fries, an assortment of
fruits and vegetables, and a large half-sour pickle. With a
gleam in her eye, Maggie picked up the pickle and, gazing
into Barrett's eyes, licked the end of it with her pink tongue.

"You're deliberately teasing me," Barrett said, his voice
suddenly breathy and hoarse.

"What's the problem with that?" Maggie asked, still licking the pickle.

Barrett reached out and grabbed her arm. "Nothing. Ab-
solutely nothing," he said as he took a big bite out of the
end of the pickle. Maggie held out a strawberry and Barrett
nibbled the end of it, while holding a slice of pineapple for
her to suck on.

She drew the pineapple slice into her mouth and with it,
Barrett's fingers. Her tongue danced over his fingertips and
her eyes locked with his. "You are a witch, you know," he
said. "I would have sworn that I couldn't feel as capable as
I do right now with a prostitute." He looked shocked, then
added, "I'm sorry. I didn't mean to insult you."

Maggie sat back in her chair. "You didn't. I enjoy sex and
now I get paid for it. I'm glad you're feeling capable because

I'm getting really hungry." She stood up, unzipped the back of her dress and let it fall to the floor and pool around her feet. She was wearing a tiny wisp of a strapless black bra, panties that were little more than a crotch panel and a few strings, a black garter belt, and stockings. "Interested in playing a bit?"

Barrett just stared as Maggie walked around to his side of the table and sat down on his lap. "I'd love to play with you," she continued, "but only if you're comfortable."

With a groan, Barrett grabbed the back of her head and pulled her down. "I'm not a bit comfortable, but I will be soon." He pressed his mouth against hers and kissed her, tangling his tongue with hers. As they kissed and he slanted his head for better contact, Maggie thought he was becoming surprisingly forceful and decisive. He completely controlled the kiss and eventually slipped his hands up her ribs to cup her bra-covered breasts. He pulled his head back and moaned, "Take all this off." As they stood, he said, "Leave the stockings and belt on. They are really hot."

Quickly he dragged off his clothes as Maggie removed her underwear. He stripped the covers off the bed and they stretched out across it. "God, I never imagined the evening would end up like this," he said. Maggie just smiled as he pressed his body against hers. She slid her hands up and down his back and flanks and finally touched his erection. He was hard and ready.

With her hands she urged him over her as she spread her legs. Although she wasn't urgently hungry, she felt so good about being with Barrett that she knew she was wet and ready. As he supported his weight on one elbow, she took his other hand and together they reached between her legs and found the slippery center of her sex. "Touch me there," she whispered. She guided his fingers to her clit and positioned his middle finger on her spot. "Here," she purred.

"Like this." She moved his hand as she climbed toward her own orgasm. Quickly she dropped her hand as his fingers learned her needs. He quickly found other places that made her moan and undulate her hips. "I need you inside me."

He thrust his penis into her hot, wet channel as he continued to rub her clit. Her breathing had speeded up and she knew that she was close to coming. "Feel it," she moaned. "Hold still inside me and just feel."

Following her instructions his body stilled, his cock lodged fully inside of her. As he kept rubbing she felt the pressure build, then explode. "Now, feel. Feel what it's like for me to come with your hard cock inside me." She felt the spasms of her orgasm grip his cock, contracting and squeezing him.

"Oh, God, Maggie," he moaned as, without any additional movement, he spurted inside of her. He collapsed, his hands now softly stroking her arm. Panting, he said, "I've never felt anything like that. You came. I could feel you."

"I know. I love coming like that, so I can feel every movement, too. It's almost like I'm caressing you with my body."

"You can't fake that, can you."

Maggie cupped his face and gazed into his eyes. "Not a chance. You did that for me."

"You're one hell of a woman, Maggie."

Maggie returned to the present as Ellen said, from across the kitchen table, "That was something. It must have made him feel ten feet tall that you came. I would guess that women can't fake that. You didn't fake anything, did you?"

"Nope. It was a joint experience and we had promised complete honesty after all." Maggie slumped back in her chair, almost as drained as she had been after sex. "I found in the years that followed that honesty in sex is probably the most important thing there is, even for a prostitute."

"Didn't you ever fake it or lie to make some customer feel good?"

Maggie sighed. "I guess I did, but somehow I don't consider them lies, just ego boosters. In general, I told the truth to everyone, most importantly myself."

"Telling yourself the truth is basic."

Maggie leaned forward and grasped Ellen's hands. "Have you been telling yourself the truth about Kevin?"

"I walked into that one, didn't I? Maybe not. If I were to be completely honest I would admit that he intrigues me and I'm really curious about what might be. Anyway, I'm sure he's only looking for a model. I'm probably building all this up in my mind."

Maggie's dark eyebrow arched again. "Maybe not."

Ellen took a deep breath. "Maybe not."

"So you're going to pose for him?"

At that moment, Ellen knew. "I am, and the devil take the hindmost."

Maggie's laugh was warm. "Don't let Lucy hear you say that."

Ellen joined the laughter. "Right."

CHAPTER 9

Later that morning Maggie noticed the new clock and the flowers sitting on an end table in a water glass. "You've moved in," she said.

"I guess I have," Ellen said with a small smile.

That afternoon they picked out a cut-glass vase and a small lamp for Ellen's dresser. Maggie also insisted that Ellen buy three pillar candles with holders for the bedroom and a CD of dance music in case a date came back to her apartment. "Not likely," Ellen had protested, but she made the purchases anyway.

Despite all her talk, Ellen changed her mind a dozen times. She couldn't possibly. She certainly could. Why should she take the risk? Why not? She hadn't gone to class on Wednesday, afraid to face Kevin, but lying in bed that night she tried to create the scene. What would it be like? Would he be tender, demanding, hesitant, forceful? Would he undress her or would she have to take off her clothes in that huge room?

Would he be a good lover? She stopped herself, sure that if she built it all up in her mind she'd be disappointed with the reality. *Afterward,* she thought, *when nothing happens I can dream about what might have been.* All Thursday morning she thought about nothing but the afternoon's modeling session.

At one o'clock she stood in her bedroom, the wispy underwear that Lucy had given her on the bed. Would it seem like an invitation? Would he misunderstand? Was it a misunderstanding? Damn. She picked up the lingerie and put it on. Then, before she could change her mind, covered it with a pair of well-washed jeans and a soft, wheat-colored flannel shirt. She added socks and loafers then reached for her navy windbreaker. *Why not something new and more stylish?* she asked herself. *Because this outfit makes me feel more comfortable,* she answered, *and I need all the support I can get.*

She walked out into the cold and windy New York fall afternoon and headed for The Templeton Gallery. By the time she had walked the few blocks, her cheeks were pink and her fingers chilled. As she opened the door, a small bell sounded and a nice-looking man who appeared to be a smaller version of Kevin bustled to the front, dressed in what she now assumed was the store uniform, casual, well-washed, black jeans and a soft cranberry shirt. "Good afternoon. May I be of assistance?"

This must be Kevin's brother. "Hi. I'm here to see Kevin."

"You must be Ellen. He's upstairs. He's been pacing all morning, afraid you wouldn't come."

"Really?"

He looked chagrined. "I'm probably not supposed to tell you but he's really excited about painting you." He closed his mouth with a snap. "In my brain and out my mouth." He cupped her chin and turned her face left and right with small humming noises. "He's right, you know. You've got great bones and there's a wonderful quality about your expression." He paused and, as she frowned, he dropped his hand. "I'm sorry to be so forward, but we're really informal around here. I'm Kevin's brother, Sean, and I play with clay. I'd love for you to pose for me sometime, too."

Ellen looked down at her ordinary body. "Why me? I don't get it. I'm nothing special, no supermodel or anything."

"Supermodels have no appeal to true artists. We like women with substance." He paused. "Oops, that didn't come out the way I'd planned. I hope you'll accept my apology."

"For what?"

She saw that he was actually blushing. "I intimated that you're not so slim."

"Well, I'm not. Does that please an artist's eye?"

"For Kev and me it does. We've studied in Europe where they don't seem to have the incredible passion for bones and skin with nothing between. The old masters loved women with flesh on their bones. It's warm, soft and," he added as he took her hand, "sexy." He lifted her hand to his lips and kissed the back.

"Oh," Ellen said, not quite knowing whether he was making a pass at her. These brothers were quite a pair. "I think I'll just go upstairs and see where Kevin is."

"Right." He dropped her hand and took a step backward. "I hope you'll seriously consider posing for me sometime, too."

"I'll certainly think about it." Ellen wondered how much time the brothers spent in that upstairs studio with lonely women who took art classes to while away idle time. Was that what she was doing? Ellen shook off the negative thoughts. Who cared why she was there, she just was.

She climbed to the upper floor where Kevin was working,

his back to her. He was dressed in casual black pants and a shirt the color of new grass. To her surprise he was barefoot. The studio smelled of chemicals and paint and music played somewhere in the background. She recognized the work as Mozart, but had no idea the name or number. She walked up behind Kevin and peered over his shoulder at the sketchbook propped on his easel. "That's me!" she gasped.

Kevin jumped, placed his hand on his chest and let out a deep breath. "*Phew*, you startled me. When I get to working, I'm afraid I become a bit deaf so I didn't hear you come in." He took another breath. "It is you, sort of."

Ellen stared. The naked woman on the pad definitely had her face, captured with a few quick strokes of Kevin's pencil. The body, however, was classically lovely with soft curves and shadowed hollows. "Oh, I wish my body looked like that."

"I hope you don't mind my taking a bit of painter's license. I have no real idea what your body looks like under all those clothes, so I just let my imagination wander." He took her hands and bussed her cheek. "I'm so glad you decided to pose."

"I'm not so sure you need me. I like the way I look on your page better than the real thing." She realized that she had reflexively clutched her jacket tightly around her.

"You're embarrassed," Kevin said, "and I'm so sorry. I didn't intend to put you off." He took her hand and kissed her palm. "Please tell me you forgive me."

Ellen burst out laughing. He was so overly sincere that it became a bit saccharin. "You're quite something," she said, her lack of belief obvious.

Kevin joined her laughter. "Okay. Busted. My technique usually works. Please. Let me take your coat. Honestly, I didn't intend to offend or embarrass."

Honestly. Ellen heard Maggie's words. Be honest with

yourself. "Honestly I am a bit embarrassed. I'm not used to men thinking about me without clothes." She pointed to the sketch. "I wish I looked like that."

"I'm glad you look just like you do and I'm so happy that you decided to come here this afternoon. Are you willing to disrobe or shall we begin with your face?"

Ellen took a deep breath. "Let's begin with the face and see how comfortable I can get with all this."

For almost an hour Kevin sketched while they talked. From time to time he changed her position on the old-fashioned burgundy velvet sofa that he had pulled to the center of the room. Finally he walked to where she was sitting. "Are you tired? You've been holding still for quite a while."

"I'm okay."

"You're being wonderfully patient with me." He stood, towering above her. "Could I unbutton a few of those buttons? I'd love to get an idea of your skin tone." When she didn't object, he reached down and slowly pushed three bone buttons through the buttonholes on the front of her shirt. His knuckles brushed her skin making her shiver. "Your skin is so warm," he purred, parting the sides of her blouse.

Suddenly Ellen couldn't concentrate, couldn't think at all. "You've got such beautiful, soft skin," he said, stroking his index finger down her breastbone to the valley between her breasts. Then he walked back to his sketch pad and picked up his pencil. "You know what I'd like you to do when you're comfortable?" His voice was soft and it was almost as if Ellen could feel it caress her.

"What?" she asked, breathless.

"I'd like you to finish unbuttoning your shirt and take it off. Would you do that for me?"

Almost without conscious thought, Ellen opened the lower buttons and pulled the shirt down her arms. The room was comfortably warm, yet she had goose bumps. How could she do this? Yet somehow she was and, trying to be honest with herself, she liked the way he was looking at her. She told herself that he was probably a total phoney, but right now he was concentrating on her, directing all his charisma at her like a searchlight. Did she mind? Not at all.

"You look as good as I thought you would and I love that sexy bit of lace you've got on." He made a few quick lines on his paper, then said, "Would you go further?" He approached again and slid one finger under her bra strap. "How far would you go?" He pulled the strap down over her shoulder until the fabric slipped off her breast. Slowly, his finger stroking across her skin, he found the other strap and slipped it off. "So beautiful," he purred. "I knew you'd be beautiful."

His look said she was beautiful and that was enough for Ellen. She reached behind her and unfastened the bra and dropped it behind the sofa with surprisingly steady hands.

"Yes," he said. He ran one finger down the curve of her breast. "So lovely. I wonder how you taste." He knelt beside the sofa and flicked his tongue over her erect nipple. Then he licked the other, and blew on the wet skin until her breast swelled and the nipple contracted to an almost painful nub. "Yes. Like that. Like a Venus preparing to meet her lover."

Some small part of her brain wondered how many women he had seduced on this sofa with exactly the same words, yet she didn't care. This was *her* experience. He was just window dressing. She reclined on the slightly threadbare sofa, stripped to the waist and felt sexy and desirable and who cared why. She watched as he returned to his easel and, with an almost fevered intensity, slashed his pencil across the paper. Slowly she toed off her loafers and pulled off her socks.

She felt like another person, and loved it. She slowly got to her feet and, as he gazed heatedly at her, unfastened the waist of her jeans and lowered the zipper. Kevin dropped his charcoal on the ledge of his easel and just stared as she hooked her thumbs in the waistband and pulled the jeans over her hips and down her legs. Finally she stood wearing just the tiny panties. "You have fooled me entirely," Kevin said.

"I have? How?"

"I thought you a tiny mouse but you are a chameleon, showing different faces to whomever looks at you." He closed the distance between them, causing her to take a step backward. "Yes," he purred. "You are at once timid and bold." He held her chin between his index finger and thumb. "And for now you are mine."

His lips closed over hers, his tongue invading, searching, taking. Ellen had never been kissed the way he was kissing her. It involved her entire body, not just her mouth, causing her knees to buckle, her nipples to tingle and molten heat to flow through her belly. She braced her hands against his chest and only his arms around her ribs kept her from collapsing. Then, in one quick move, he swept her up and lay her on the sofa. As she watched, he pulled off his clothes until he stood, gloriously naked.

He was gorgeous, his skin well tanned and covered with heavy, dark hair, his shoulders broad, his hips narrow. As she gazed at him, her eyes were drawn down through the whorls of hair on his chest and the narrow strip over his belly to the black nest of his rampant erection. He was huge and Ellen was sure that nothing that size could ever enter her body. Yet his smile was confident as his gaze caressed her as hers caressed him. Carefully he removed her panties and pushed her legs apart until one foot rested on the floor, and one on the sofa back. Then he crouched between her knees. "You knew this was going to happen, just as I did. Tell me you want it as much as I do."

Ellen took a deep breath. Honesty. "I do. I'm just a little scared. I've never done anything like this before."

Kevin combed his long fingers through her pubic hair. "I can take away all your fears." His fingers found her, slipping over her already sopping flesh. Then he bent over and his mouth followed his fingers. "I love the taste of a woman's body." His tongue found every fold of her, licking and stroking everywhere she hungered. She threaded her fingers through his long hair and held on tightly, keeping his head between her legs. She was being driven higher and higher by his talented mouth.

Then he did two things that drove her over the edge. Almost simultaneously he filled her with two fingers and his mouth found her clit and sucked. She screamed as an orgasm slammed through her. She realized in some still-aware place, that it was the first time she had come without her own hands touching her body.

She felt him leave her momentarily and heard the telltale ripping of a condom package. Then he was back, his giant cock driving into her, filling her body, pushing her open, more aware of him than she had been of any man.

Again she felt the waves, the convulsions of her channel against his penis. "Yes, Ellen, oh yes." Then he was incapable of speech as he bellowed and came inside of her. Yet even as his orgasm took him, he didn't stop playing with her clit. His mouth moved to a turgid nipple and he bit down lightly. Again she felt orgasm crash over her, spasms taking her, making her claw at Kevin's shoulders.

Finally her body quieted and Kevin stretched out beside her so she could feel the pounding of his heart. "That was amazing," he said, his voice hoarse. "I've never met a more responsive woman."

Ellen had never experienced anything like making love with Kevin. Her body was exhausted, satiated, yet fresh and new. She giggled. "I'm so happy I want to laugh out loud." And when she did Kevin joined her.

"I knew when you showed up that we would end up here," Kevin said. "I've been dreaming about it all week."

"If I were being honest, I knew it, too."

Lazily he stroked along her hip, yet Ellen felt his sudden intensity. "Will you come back again soon? Tomorrow?"

"Kevin, this is all very new to me. Let's take it slowly, okay?"

"I don't want to go slowly. I want to devour you six times a day. I want to make love to you in every possible way."

Ellen held his gaze and tried to put her feelings into words. "I need to keep this all in perspective. Today was wonderful, amazing, like nothing that's ever been for me before and I don't want to spoil it. I want to go slowly. Please."

"How can I do that when every time I look at you I will see and feel what we've had this afternoon?"

More Kevin Duffy patented charisma? Did he say this to every woman he made love to on this sofa? Who cared? It would burn hot, but she'd try to tame the flame if she possibly could.

"I want to be able to attend your art classes without feeling like the blue-plate special. I don't know whether it's possible, but let's at least make an effort to keep everything in its place. I need to come to class tomorrow morning and see whether I can concentrate on painting with you in the room. I hope I can since I don't want to find another teacher . . . for anything." When he started to say something, Ellen covered his lips with her fingers. "I also want to continue what we've done here. Do you really want to paint me or was that just a convenient way to get me up here alone?"

Kevin let out a quick breath and nodded. "I actually want to paint you."

"Maybe one afternoon next week. You can paint, and then, if we both want to, we can indulge in other passions."

"You are a difficult woman, but sensible. Come to class tomorrow. I can't be with you over the weekend. That's when the gallery is busy and I've got other commitments. Can you be here with me Tuesday afternoon? You can pose, and whatever." His leer was so exaggerated that she grinned. He continued, "Having to wait until Tuesday will make the weekend go slowly, but I will know I have something to look forward to as well."

Ellen wondered whether she could juggle her feelings as well as she had just told Kevin she could. She wanted to make love with him over and over. It felt like a drug, making her crave more and more yet she wouldn't allow herself to become addicted. She was too new at all this. "Yes. Tuesday afternoon."

Ellen wandered home in a daze and, as she had half expected, found Maggie waiting for her in the kitchen, an open bottle of wine and two half-filled glasses on the table. "I know where you've been, but I didn't eavesdrop, I promise, although I will admit that, if I could have, I'd have been really tempted. Want to talk?"

Ellen dropped her jacket on the counter and sunk, exhausted and drained, onto a chair. She took several swallows of the wine. "Wow. This is sensational. Did you bring it?"

"I did. I've no idea how it is that sometimes I can walk into a store and appear just like any other person, but I brought this to celebrate or commiserate." She raised her ever-inquisitive eyebrow. "Well? Which is it?"

Ellen couldn't suppress a grin. "Celebrate. It was fantastic, toe-curling, earth-moving sex."

"I'd love to hear as many details as you want to tell," Maggie said, "but I'd be content with just the look on your face." She hesitated, then slammed her palm on the table. "Like hell I would. Tell, woman!"

Ellen told Maggie many of the details of the afternoon, omitting only those that were too personal, both to her and to Kevin. "It was astounding."

"So, you're in love."

"With Kevin? Not at all. I do think that I'm in love with good sex, however."

"You're in lust and you're a very smart woman to know the difference. Bravo!"

"Thanks. I hope I can live up to my big talk."

"I think you can," Maggie said, finishing her wine, standing up and squeezing Ellen's shoulder. "I'll leave you to your sketching and your fantasies. I'll be in touch soon, I guess. I don't think Angela and Lucy are through with us yet."

"I'm glad." Ellen stood and gave Maggie a heartfelt hug. "You've become very important to me."

Maggie returned the hug. "That goes double for me." She left the kitchen and Ellen heard the front door close behind her. She picked up her wine and sipped. Maggie had given her several lessons in wine and now she was able to appreciate the bouquet, the color, the myriad of flavors. In the kitchen, she opened the closet over the counter where she kept several bottles of wine. She pulled out all the ones with screw caps and put them in a bag beside her garbage can. "Out with the old, and in with the new."

Filled with enthusiasm for life and all parts of it, she walked into the wine store in which she and Maggie had bought her first bottle. The same clerk was standing behind the counter waiting on an older couple. She walked to the wine rack on which she had found that first special bottle and studied, now better able to understand the labels. "Yes, of course," he said, walking up behind her. "The Mount Eden Estate." He nodded and looked impressed. "Was it as good as I've heard? I've never actually tasted it."

"Yes, it was. Great nose, fabulous color, and all the ripe fruit you could want. It was a great choice, but that was for a special occasion. I'm interested in something now that won't disappoint, but that's not quite so pricey."

By the time she and the salesclerk finished she had two bottles of white and two of red, and she had held her own with the clerk. Her. Ellen Harold, girl wine enthusiast. Small-town woman in the big city. She was learning.

That evening, Ellen daydreamed, reliving her wonderful afternoon with Kevin, and did some sketching. She had been to the local branch of the library and selected several books on drawing and painting. She had read that, although she needed to get out and find places to paint, she could do some landscapes from pictures or from her imagination. In the library's extensive video section she had taken out a travel tape of Hawaii, thinking that the unusual vistas would give her inspiration. As she sat on the sofa with the remote control in her hand, the phone rang. Absently she picked it up, expecting to hear her sister Micki's voice. "Hello?"

"Hello, Ellen. It's Jim."

Ellen hit the pause button and dropped the remote on the sofa beside her. "Well, it's so nice to hear from you," she said, wondering how she could hear his voice over the pounding of her heart. After their dinner together the previous weekend, she had been enthused about seeing him again, but when he didn't call for several days she assumed she wouldn't hear from him again.

"I said I'd call you in a week or so but I must admit that

I got impatient. If you're not busy this weekend, maybe we could have dinner again, this time my treat." He rushed on. "Of course if you're busy I'll understand. Maybe we could do it some other time."

"Whoa," Ellen said, stopping the onrushing words. "This weekend would be fine. How about Saturday?" Was this really her? Ellen asked herself. She was being so much more aggressive than she had ever been. Maybe it was because he was being so tentative, unsure, so sweet and shy, exactly the opposite of Kevin.

"Oh. Saturday would be great. I was thinking, well, have you ever had Japanese food?"

"You mean sushi? Raw fish? I don't think I could." She didn't think she was that brave.

"Actually there is a small, really fine restaurant called Senbazuru right around the corner from where we ate last week. It has tempura and sukiyaki as well as sushi and sashimi. You could have cooked food and I could have what I like."

Ellen heard Maggie's words. *Have you ever tasted sushi?* "That sounds terrific. What time shall I meet you?"

"Still not comfortable with telling me where you live, I see." When she started to protest, he said quickly, "That's fine. Eventually I hope you'll decide that I'm just a lonely guy questing an attractive woman to spend time with."

Cordless phone in her hand, Ellen stood and walked into the bathroom and stared at herself in the mirror. Not so attractive, she thought, but not half bad. Maggie was right. It was the attitude. "What time?"

"How about seven," Jim said and gave her the address of the restaurant. They talked for a few more minutes, then hung up. Ellen lay back on the sofa, unable to suppress a grin. She had a date with Jim. And another date with Kevin for sex. Shit. She thought of the seventies song. She was woman, hear her roar. "*Roar!*"

The following morning was Friday and she knew that Kevin was holding class. She really wanted to attend so, taking her courage in both hands, she grabbed her paint box and headed off. Surprisingly, she took her place at an easel with little awkwardness and got to work quickly. Kevin was professional and only as attentive to her as he was to the other students. Just before the class ended he walked up behind her and whispered, "I wish we were alone."

From that moment on work became impossible. As she was leaving, he said, "I hope I didn't ruin your concentration."

Her mind had filled with images of what they had been doing in that very room the previous afternoon. She blushed. "You did, just a bit but I did manage to get some good work done."

"I'm amazed that I managed to concentrate, but I did, too. Will you be here Tuesday?"

Ellen's blush deepened. "I think so."

"I hope so."

Friday evening, after an afternoon of reading about art and working with her paints, she made herself a pot of macaroni and cheese, watched some TV, and then settled in the bathtub. She had lit a few candles and poured a capful of a new body oil beneath the spigot and placed the CD player on the counter. Now her head was filled with erotic images of Kevin and Jim, the sound of clarinets and the voice of the narrator of the sensual tales of magic and power.

CHAPTER 10

"Is there magic in the world? Skeptics doubt that magic exists, or ever did exist. Are they right? I don't know, but there are still a few people who are willing to keep an open mind, people who believe in old stories, ancient legends, and possibilities. Like the possibilities inherent in the Mask of Invisibility.

"Ben had lived on the same block most of his life. Several years before, when he was nineteen, an adult club called the Pleasure Parlor had set up shop several doors down from his apartment building and since then, every time Ben passed he gazed at the mysterious-looking doorway. LIVE SEX ACTS the sign read. 'See it all happen right before your eyes.' If he only could just slip inside and see what all the fuss was about.

"It wasn't that he didn't have girlfriends. Right now Sue was his steady and he had found himself actually think-

ing about marriage. Yet, they hadn't had great sex. It was good with Sue but there were no rockets, no fireworks, no earthquakes. Was it just that he hadn't found the right woman, or did that kinky stuff only exist in Playboy *and XXX-rated movies? Was there something wrong with him or with her? Would she be interested in something a bit more acrobatic? He'd probably never know.*

"One evening on his way home from an evening with Sue, he passed the Pleasure Parlor. 'Come on in! You know you want to see what goes on inside,' the guy standing at the doorway said. 'Only ten bucks.'

" 'Not tonight,' Ben said, as he'd said at least once a week since the club opened.

" 'Why not, buddy? Lots to see.' The guy, an over-developed, muscle beach type winked at him. 'Lots!'

" 'Not tonight,' Ben repeated and walked on. What if one of his friends or neighbors saw him walking into that place or worse, saw him inside, utterly fascinated? He couldn't risk the embarrassment.

"Several strides later, he heard, Psst. *He whirled around and saw a tiny woman bundled into a heavy brown coat and woolen scarf, signaling him from a doorway. 'I know that you really want to get inside,' she said, 'and I can help you.'*

" 'Sorry,' Ben said, turning back toward his building. 'Not interested.'

" 'Sure you are,' the woman said, walking up beside him and placing her hand on his arm. 'Things go on in there that you might never see anywhere else.'

"Shit, *Ben thought.* Another come-on. These places will use anything to get a guy to pay ten bucks to get inside. *'I'm really not interested but thanks anyway.'*

" 'Listen. This isn't a come-on. I just want you to see the sights. It's truly educational.' "

"Ben tried to remove the woman's hand from his arm, but her grip was surprisingly strong. 'Please, lady.' He tried to get a better look at the woman but the coat covered her body completely and her face was almost hidden beneath her scarf.

"The woman grinned. 'Lady. That's rich.' She moved in front of him and stared directly into his eyes. 'Listen, Ben, it's this way . . .'

" 'How do you know my name?'

" 'I just do. It's my job. Anyway, I know what you want. I know what you need.' She pulled a slender piece of black cloth from her pocket. 'This is the Mask of Invisibility. Put it on and you can go inside and experience what's there for you. No money, no embarrassment, no nothing.'

"Ben stared at the Lone Ranger–type black domino dangling from the woman's fingers. 'Okay, what's the angle here?'

" 'No angle. I just want this for you. If you're going to think about marriage to Sue, you need to know what else there is in the world.'

" 'How did you . . . ?'

" 'Don't worry about trivialities. I am giving you the opportunity of a lifetime here. Stop arguing.'

"Ben was intrigued. 'How much?'

" 'No charge. You get to use it until tomorrow morning. After that, it becomes just a piece of cloth.'

" 'Right. Sure. You really expect me to believe this bull?'

" 'It's not bull. Take the mask and put it on. Walk up to Artie there by the door and see whether he asks you for any money.'

" 'Maybe this is some kind of sick joke the two of you cooked up.'

"The woman's shoulders rose and lowered in a long, drawn-out sigh. 'Okay. Go into the all-night drugstore, the supermarket, whatever. Pick up something and walk out without paying. You'll see that this really works.'

" 'Why me?'

" 'Let's just say I'm a guardian angel. Does that make it any easier to understand?'

"He shook his head. 'Not really.'

"The woman pressed the cloth into Ben's hand and said, 'Just use it and you'll see everything. And no one will see you.' She cackled at her little joke and disappeared. Just vanished into nothingness. One minute she was standing holding Ben's arm, and the next she was gone. A voice whispered into Ben's ear, 'One more thing. Tell Sue about what you see. You'll be very surprised.'

"Ben whirled around but the sidewalk was empty. The only reminder he had of the woman's presence was the black mask in his hand. This is all ridiculous, *he told himself* as he balled the domino up in his fist and headed for a sidewalk trash can. And yet. . . .

"With his hand suspended over the trash he looked at his fist and the cloth inside. He had always operated on the 'what's in it for me' principle and he couldn't figure out what was in this silliness for the woman. Why had she given this to him? It had to be some kind of elaborate practical joke, but why?

"When he couldn't come up with an answer, he decided to play along, at least for a few minutes to see what would happen. He walked several blocks to an all-night convenience store, tied the mask on and slipped inside, afraid he'd be taken for a stickup man.

"He walked around the store, seemingly unnoticed.

Several people stood on the checkout line as he picked up a six-pack and stood behind a tall, heavyset man with a magazine and a large bottle of soda. 'Thank you, sir,' the clerk said to the tall man as he finished paying for his items. Then the clerk turned away and began to rearrange the cartons of cigarettes as though there was no one else in line. Ben put his beer on the counter but there was still no reaction.

"*He looked down at himself and to him there seemed to be no difference. He could see himself perfectly, but the clerk was completely ignoring him. 'Sir,' he said. 'I'd like to pay for my beer.' There was no reaction from behind the counter. 'Sir!' Nothing.*

"*He turned and glanced at a mirrored sign. He wasn't there. He waved his free hand at himself, or rather where he should be in the mirror, but there was nothing reflected. No Ben, no beer, no nothing. He lifted his hand from the six-pack and it suddenly appeared on the counter but he still wasn't visible. The clerk turned, looked around with a puzzled expression on his face, then picked up the six-pack and replaced it on a stack beside the counter. Then he returned to his cigarette stacking.*

"*Hmmm. Interesting. It seemed as if the mask worked. No one could see him. Amazing.* So what are you waiting for, *he asked himself. He dashed out of the convenience store and headed toward the Pleasure Parlor. Finally he'd see what went on inside and no one would be the wiser. None of his friends or neighbors would be able to see him.*

"*He walked up to Mr. Bodybuilder, still hawking the Pleasure Parlor's attractions and looked him right in the eye, his face inches from the bouncer's. Nothing. Ben shook his head in wonderment and walked through the* black curtains. The air was thick with smoke and the room was so poorly lit that at first he could see very little. It smelled of tobacco and sweat and the pungent odor of sex. The music was almost deafening, pounding drums, the rhythm unmistakable.

"He looked around and saw that the audience was entirely male. At the front of the room there was a small stage where two women, wearing only G-strings, danced to the exaggerated beat. As Ben's eyes adjusted he saw that they were not bad-looking. They had nice figures with large breasts and prominent nipples. On one side a redhead was grinding her hips, her hands rubbing her crotch suggestively. On the other, a brunette was gyrating against a brass pole, pressing her large tits against the metal.

" 'Bring on the stud,' someone in the audience yelled. The chant of 'Stud, Stud,' was picked up by others in the room.

"Finally a man in a tux walked out onto the stage. 'You want Stud?'

" 'Yeah,' screamed the men in the audience.

" 'Say it again,' Tux yelled.

" 'Stud!' the men screamed.

" 'Okay. Anyone want to leave?'

" 'No!'

"Ben wondered who Stud was, but whatever was going to happen he was ready. He walked up to the stage and perched on the edge, invisible to everyone in the room.

" 'Okay,' Tux said. 'Lock the doors!' Several men walked to the exits and, with exaggerated motions, closed and locked the doors. 'No cops in here tonight!'

" 'Stud! Stud! Stud!' There were whistles and feet stomped. The rhythmic clapping was almost deafening.

" 'All right. Let's bring on Stud.' Tux left the stage and the two women faced the opening in the burgundy curtain across the back. Suddenly the curtain parted and a man stepped out. He was dressed in black pants and black cowboy boots. A small black vest covered with silver conchos barely concealed his well-muscled, naked chest. He wore wide leather wristlets, a wide, black leather band around his forehead, and his long hair was tied with a black leather thong.

"Ben had never cared about looking at other men, but this guy was the hunkiest, sexiest guy he'd ever seen. Although Ben knew it was all just an act, it certainly appeared that the two women were staring at Stud with hunger in their eyes.

"As the man walked toward the front of the stage, Ben got a good look at his face, deep brown, piercing eyes, a wide sensual mouth, and a gold hoop earring in each ear. There was something of the pirate about him, lusty and pure male. Stud looked at the redhead and said, 'Stay there. I'll get to you later.' Then he crossed to the brunette who was standing, her back against the brass pole. Without a word, he grabbed her wrists and pulled them sharply behind her around the pole. He pulled off his headband and bound her arms. With her shoulders pulled backward, her large breasts pressed forward, her nipples hugely erect.

"Down,' Stud said and the brunette slid down the pole until she was on her knees. The man grabbed her tits and pushed them together, then rubbed the front of his pants against the cleft between them. With thrusts of his hips, he fucked her tits. 'Great boobs,' he said. 'Who wants them?'

" 'Me!' several voices from the audience said.

"Stud looked over the audience, then pointed to a

man on one side of the room. As the man stood and made his way between the tightly packed tables and onto the stage, Ben could see that he was of average height and build, wearing slacks and a button-down shirt. 'She's yours,' Stud said. 'Let's see what you can do with her.' The man unzipped his pants and pulled out his already erect cock. He pressed the brunette's large tits together and rubbed his cock in her shadowy valley.

"Stud reached to a man at a front table and took his beer glass. Slowly he poured the liquid over the woman's breasts until the man threw back his head and bellowed as come spurted from his cock. Applause filled the room and Stud yelled, 'Later for the rest of you.' The sound in the room grew to deafening proportions.

"As the exhausted man left the stage to return to his seat, Stud crossed to the redhead. He pointed to her crotch. 'You were bad,' he growled. 'I saw you. You watched Tina's boobs and you touched yourself.' The woman hung her head. 'Do it again.' The redhead rubbed her crotch with both hands, her face obviously enjoying the feel of her hands.

" 'That's very bad.' He opened the ties at the side of her G-string and pulled it off. Ben stared at her red bush, neatly trimmed to a small triangle. Stud motioned again and the redhead buried her fingers in the curly red thatch. Stud allowed her to continue for a moment, watching her obvious excitement, then slapped her hands. 'Bad!'

"The cry was taken up by the audience. 'Bad! Bad! Bad!'

"Stud looked at the men. 'What should I do?'

" 'Punish her! Punish her! Punish her!'

"A man at the front of the room grabbed his chair and hoisted it up onto the stage. Then Tux walked out with a short, brown leather crop.

" 'Do it! Do it! Do it!'

"It seemed to Ben that, although the woman tried to appear frightened, her eyes shone with lust as she stared at the crop. Ben was amazed. This was all new to him. He'd read stories and seen pictures, of course, but here he was in the middle of a real scene. This was really happening, and it seemed as if the redhead wanted it. Badly. Ben found that his palm itched and the urge to slap her was almost irresistible. As the woman draped herself over Stud's lap, Ben could almost feel the sting of his hand against her bottom. Shit. His cock was suddenly harder than he'd ever imagined. He looked over the crowd to reassure himself that no one could see him, then unzipped his pants and took out his raging hard-on.

"As Stud raised the crop, Ben wrapped his hand around his cock. The crop whistled through the air and came down across the redhead's buttocks. She bucked and screamed but from this close Ben could tell she was getting hotter and hotter. Again and again the crop landed on her buttocks, leaving red stripes across white flesh. Tears filled her eyes, and yet she didn't move, didn't try to evade the sting of the crop. It was obvious to Ben that she was enjoying it all.

" 'Eight . . . nine . . . ten!' the audience yelled.

" 'That's enough for tonight,' Stud said, 'as long as you're a good girl from now on.' He pushed her onto her haunches and unzipped his pants. His cock was huge, bigger than anything Ben had ever seen. He leered at the redhead as he rubbed his erection. 'Suck.'

"*Greedily she took him in her hand, then opened her mouth and drew in about half of him. Her hand covered the rest as her head bobbed against his groin. Over and over she pulled back, then took him in. Finally, he pushed her away and, with the men watching, spurted come all over the woman's face. Grinning, she licked her lips, then scooped up the come with her fingers and licked.*

"*Ben was close to coming himself, but he decided to take advantage of his invisibility once more. He climbed onto the stage and approached the brunette, still on her knees, tied to the pole. Would she feel him? He lifted her magnificent breasts and buried his cock between them. He looked into her confused face. She could feel him, but she hadn't any idea what she was feeling. Suddenly her hands were free and she was holding her breasts, her head thrown back, a look of pure joy on her face. Ben pinched her nipples and thrust his cock between her slippery tits. As he pinched harder, the brunette's face contorted and she used one hand to rub her crotch.*

"*He came. He had wanted it to last, but it was impossible. As the come left his cock and landed on the brunette's chest, he could see it become visible. Then the woman screamed, obviously in the throes of a violent orgasm. Stud walked over and hissed, 'That's not part of the show. You're supposed to come with one of the paying customers.'*

"*She panted, then said, 'I don't know what came over me but it was as though someone was fucking my tits and pinching my nipples. You know how I get when anyone does that.'*

" *'There's no one here,' Stud whispered.*

" *'I know. It was just so real.'*

"*Ignoring the brunette's orgasm, Stud looked out over the sea of men's faces. 'Okay, guys.' He pointed to several men, 'Your turn.'*

"*Ben caught his breath and made his way to the door. He quickly unlocked it and, totally exhausted, headed home.*

"*The following evening, he met Sue at her apartment. As the woman had promised, the mask had become just a piece of black cloth that morning. He had put it on and had seen himself quite clearly in the mirror, looking like a poor-man's Lone Ranger. He had spent the rest of the day reliving the previous evening. Over and over he watched the redhead and the crop. Again and again he felt his cock between the brunette's tits.*

"*As he settled on the sofa with his arm around Sue, he remembered the woman's words. 'Tell Sue about what you see. You'll be very surprised.'*

" *'I had the most bizarre experience last evening.'*

" *'Really?' Sue said, her eyes sparkling.*

" *'Well, it's a bit difficult to explain. A woman gave me something.'*

"*Sue grinned. 'Then she found you.'*

"*Ben's head whipped around. 'Who found me?'*

" *'Sorry. Continue your story.'*

"*Ben cupped Sue's face in his palm and turned her toward him. 'Something's going on here. Tell me what you know about last evening.'*

He watched Sue try to lower her eyes but his hand held her fast. He could read guilt in her eyes.

" *'Okay. I've seen the Pleasure Parlor and I knew you wanted to see what went on inside. I thought it might give you some interesting ideas.'*

" *'What do you know about what goes on in there?'*

" *'My ex-boyfriend used to go there and he told me*

*all about it. Did you see Stud? And did he spank one
of the girls?'*

" *'Yes.'*

"Sue pulled Ben's hand away and stood. 'Well?'

" *'Well what?'*

" *'Did it turn you on?'*

*"Ben cleared his throat. Although she might not like
it, he wasn't about to lie about it. 'Yes.'*

" *'I hoped it would.' She leaned away from him and
stroked her bottom. 'Did you watch him fucking her
tits?' She rubbed her breasts, pushing them together beneath her sweater.*

" *'Yes, and before you ask, that turned me on as well.'
He watched Sue's grin widen. 'What do you know
about my guardian angel? Did you set that up somehow?'*

" *'Is that what she told you? That she was your
guardian angel?'*

*"Ben thought back. 'Actually, she said she was a
guardian angel.'*

" *'Right, silly, she's mine.' Sue sat back down and
pressed her body against Ben's.*

" *'Holy shit,' Ben said as he reached for Sue's breasts.
'Holy shit.' "*

Ellen had used her fingers to satisfy her hunger during the
story and now she pressed the stop button. Spanking for
sexual pleasure. She never would have imagined it, but the
narrator made it seem so real, so natural, just a part of good
sex. She wasn't ready for experimentation to that extent.
Was she?

She sighed, closing her eyes and enjoying the erotic images
that whirled in her head. Kevin's studio. The feel of the velvet sofa fabric beneath her naked buttocks, the smell of tur-

pentine and paint mixed with Kevin's aftershave, the feel of him filling her. Again her fingers slipped between her legs and rubbed her clit. The sound of Mozart in the background, almost drowned out by Kevin's harsh breathing, the taste of his lips. Would she have enjoyed it if he had gotten a bit rough? She didn't know but the idea didn't repel her as it might have earlier.

In her mind the scene shifted to her dinner date with Jim. How would he be as a lover? Her eyes flew open. Was she really thinking about Jim in those terms? If she were to be honest with herself, yes, she was. "And," she said aloud, "what's wrong with that?" How had she changed so much in just a few weeks? Before she met Maggie she had been smaller, shy, unwilling to experiment. What had Maggie done to her? She and Kevin had only been together once but, with the help of the erotic CD stories and with Maggie's encouragement Ellen was able to admit, to herself at least, that she was curious, anxious to see the variations that the sexual world held. Until now she had been peeking out of her cocoon. Now, although she wasn't a true butterfly yet, she was eager to give her new wings a real try.

CHAPTER 11

Over the next several weeks, Ellen's life fell into a pattern. She met with Kevin once or twice a week. He sketched and painted various views of her naked body and afterward they had great, toe-curling sex together. Neither, however, was under any delusion. This was fun and games. They cared about each other, but not in the deep, long-lasting way that would define marriage or even a semipermanent relationship.

She saw Jim every weekend. One crisp fall day they rented a car and drove through Westchester County, stopping at farm stands, drinking fresh apple cider and eating homemade doughnuts. They spent an entire day exploring the South Street Seaport area and another poking around Nyack with its quaint shops and restaurants. They took the Staten Island ferry, riding on the open deck even though the thermometer hovered close to forty degrees.

They got to know each other, too. She felt comfortable with him, relishing their time together as she used to enjoy her time with her sister. It was almost as though she had compartmentalized her life: Kevin for sex and Jim for friendship.

Between dates, Ellen did her work for the doctors in Fairmont, and sketched. She practiced the techniques she learned in Kevin's art classes and those she gleaned from books on all aspects of painting and drawing. She also watched television, went to movies, and filled her time with exploring New York. One Saturday afternoon, she and Jim saw a Saturday matinee of a smash hit musical. As they walked out of the warm theater, Jim asked, "What would you like to do now? It's a bit early for dinner."

Since they had had a large lunch, Ellen had to agree. Jim had picked her up at her apartment a few times but they had never spent any time there. The play had been a rather sensual love story and Ellen found that her sexual juices were flowing. She gazed at Jim, his soft sandy hair and thick mustache, thought about his easy smile and great sense of humor. Why was Jim always relegated to the role of friend? She looked at him as a man and found he was attractive. How would that mustache feel against her skin? she wondered.

Ellen had often considered what it would be like if Jim made a pass, but he had never stepped even the slightest bit out of line. A few good-night kisses were as far as they had gotten. Although they talked at length about their lives, no explanation had even presented itself. Was he gay? Had he been so badly burned by marriage that he wasn't interested in anything intimate? Was it her? Recently she had begun to wonder whether her newfound boldness was all an illusion. Maybe she was still the same small-town person she had been when she moved to New York. New hairdo, new clothes, new makeup, even her new sexuality didn't change the basic person she was and maybe Jim knew that. It seemed obvious that he wasn't about to make any moves, maybe it was time for her to ratchet up their relationship. "How about coming back to my apartment? We can share a bottle of wine and I think I have some cheese to nibble on. Then we can decide what to do about dinner." Ellen could see the surprise in Jim's eyes.

"I'd like that," he said.

As she let herself and Jim into her apartment, she realized that the change in it was startling. Now it was warm, with the insipid floral oils on the walls replaced with museum-quality floral prints framed in silver. The tables were covered with pots of ferns and philodendrons. Cyclamen and African violets cluttered the living room windowsill. Ellen had bought several coordinated pillows to liven up the sofa and a small Oriental rug in deep blue, cranberry, and gold lay beneath the coffee table. "Nice place," Jim said. "It's comfortable, and just right for someone like you."

"For someone like me? What does that mean?"

"I have always had the feeling that you might decide to decamp one morning and move back to Fairmont. I know you're enjoying your art classes and such, but I haven't gotten the feeling that you're here permanently. It's sort of like you have one foot here and one back home. I kind of thought that when your money ran out you'd go back to the way things were before."

"Really?"

"I've noticed that when you say the word *home* you always mean upstate. I've tried to protect myself from being too disappointed when you tell me you're going back. When you 'find yourself' I mean."

Interesting, Ellen thought. Although Jim didn't know about the extent of her lottery winnings, she had told him that she came into a bit of money and was staying in the city to find herself. She wasn't sure what 'find herself' meant, but it was a good enough phrase to explain where her head was at the moment. Where was she heading? Strangely she realized that she had no more idea about that than she had when she arrived in New York City. She was just gliding. Shouldn't there be more to life than just occupying time? "I never thought about it that way," she said aloud. "I guess I don't know what the future holds for me just yet."

She opened a bottle of Chablis and they sipped. As they sat, staring into space, Ellen wondered what he was thinking. Was he wondering how to get out of this situation gracefully? Didn't he find her attractive? "Why haven't you ever made a pass at me?" she blurted out. Better to know than to wonder.

She could hear Jim's startled intake of breath, then he just stared at the wineglass in his hand and sighed. "I've told you that I don't like getting into anything deeper when I know it's not going to last. I'm not sure I'd be good at a one-night stand."

"We're hardly one nighters. We've been seeing each other for two months."

"Okay. If I were being totally honest, I didn't want to rush things. Two months seems like a long time, but . . ."

"Is that all?" Ellen asked, feeling brave enough to continue the conversation. "Honest?"

With another loud sigh, Jim put his glass on the table. "Honesty's tough. I'm a pretty lonely guy," he began. "I don't have many friends, and most of the ones I have are men. I have enjoyed your company so much for the past weeks that I was scared of something messing that up. You were so reluctant to have me up to your apartment that I decided that you weren't interested in going further than just friendship so I forced myself to be content with that."

"You always seemed so confident. You picked me up in the store and again outside the restaurant that first night."

"My confidence is all an illusion. I saw you, alone and, I hoped, as lonely as I was, so I bucked up my courage and approached you. It turned out so great I've been afraid to mess it up by pushing things further."

Ellen put her glass beside Jim's. "What if I said I was interested in going further?" As she spoke she sensed Jim pulling away.

With a rueful grin, he said, "I would be scared to death."

"Scared? Of me?"

"You're an attractive woman. I'm sure you've had your share of men and, although you never talk about it, you probably have someone special right now." He hesitated, then plunged on. "I'm not good with women, except as friends. There was my wife, of course, but that was different. It took her two years to discover that she didn't want any more time with me. I guess there's something wrong with me. Women don't seem to continue a relationship with me once we've been to bed."

With the wine heating her belly, Ellen thought of Maggie's words. "You know," Ellen said, "I have a good friend, a woman by the way, who once told me that there aren't really any good lovers. There are people who are great together, but wouldn't necessarily be nearly as good with other partners. Good lovers come in pairs." As she spoke she realized that, thanks to Kevin, for the first time in her life she was being the sexual aggressor. It was a heady feeling.

"That's a nice theory," Jim said, his shoulders slumped, "but I'm not sure I buy it."

"Tell me, if you had a magic wand and could have anything you wanted with a woman in bed, what would you want?"

Jim moved slightly farther away from her. "Damn, you do ask the most uncomfortable questions."

"You don't have to answer, I'm just curious."

His deep breath was loud and prolonged. Then he grinned shyly. "Do I have to be honest again?"

"I wish you would be," Ellen said, unwilling to let him off the small hook she had put him on. She had learned a lot about sex from Kevin and from the stories on the CD Maggie had given her.

"That's an interesting question. A magic wand. I guess I would want her to want me as much as I wanted her." He smiled. "I'd want her to tell me what she liked so I wouldn't be trying to guess all the time." He stopped as if realizing that he might have said too much. "What made you come up with such a question?"

"I thought it would be a good way to learn about you." She remembered Maggie telling her about using the stories on the CD for communication. It just might work with Jim, if he had the open mind she thought he did. If not . . . "The same friend I mentioned earlier gave me a CD with a collection of highly erotic short stories. They are all about magic and having the power to have sex exactly the way you want it and the idea intrigued me. Actually there's a story on the CD about a man who wants to know what his girlfriend likes."

"A CD with erotic short stories? An interesting idea. I must confess that I'm a Web surfer and I read lots of porn."

Would the story totally embarrass Jim or would it open the path to good communication? According to Maggie, the ability to communicate was the most important thing for good sex. In for a penny . . . "I don't know the difference between pornography and erotica, but these stories are soft and loving. I could play it for you. I'm afraid it's really explicit." She laughed. "I'm not sure I could look at you while we listen, but I think all of the stories have valuable messages."

"I'd like to hear the one you were talking about," Jim said. Ellen retrieved her CD player from the bedroom and set it on the coffee table. She realized that it had gotten quite dark outside as the fall evening advanced so all she had to do was turn off one lamp and the room was plunged into almost complete darkness, the only illumination coming in was from the streetlights outside the window.

Jim took her hand. "It seems we've just found a mutual love for explicit tales. Okay. Play on, McDuff."

Realizing that their relationship had just passed a milestone, Ellen pressed play.

"Is there magic in the world?" the voice said as the music faded. *"Skeptics doubt that magic exists, or ever did exist. Are they right? I don't know, but there are still a few people who are willing to keep an open mind, people who believe in old stories, ancient legends, and possibilities. Like the possibilities inherent in the Cloak of Veracity.*

"Zack liked to prowl antique shops. He seldom bought anything, but he had a love of anything that had once been used, touched by people who had died long before he was born. So in stores all around the city he sat in eighteenth-century chairs, rubbed his long fingers over George V tables, even wrote a note on a French desk supposedly owned by Marie Antoinette. He felt some kind of connection to all those who had touched and sat and written before him.

"One afternoon he was browsing in a new store in a very high-class part of town when he stumbled on a soft gray cloak with elaborate gold buttons. 'What in the world is this?' he asked the bored salesman.

"The man wandered over and gazed at the cloth. 'I'm told it's the Cloak of Veracity, the very one that Merlin created so Arthur could find out what Guinevere was up to.' He laughed. 'I guess he never got to use it, huh.'

" 'Cloak of Veracity. What does it do?' Zack asked.

" 'The one who wears it is incapable of telling a lie.' As if sensing a man with money, the clerk continued, 'I'm told it's genuine.'

"Zack picked it up. 'It can't be really old,' he said. 'It's in perfect condition. No wear and tear at all.'

" 'That's one of the properties of the cloak,' the store clerk said. 'It remains in perfect condition and has throughout the ages.'

"Zack swirled the cloak around his shoulders. He started to say that he wasn't really interested in the thing, then found himself saying instead, 'How much?'

"The clerk reached up to the small collar and looked at the tag safety-pinned to it. 'It says three hundred dollars.'

" 'Okay,' Zack said, 'never mind.' He swirled the cloak like a matadore. Cloak of Veracity indeed.

" 'I could let you have it for two-fifty,' the clerk said.

"Zack let the swirling cloak land on the clerk's shoulders. 'How much?'

" 'Actually that thing has been here for more than six months and yours is the first genuine offer we've had. No one believes it's real. I'll take anything I can get over a hundred bucks.'

"Zack cocked his head to one side. 'Interesting.' He removed the cloak. This is probably some kind of scam, he thought, but it's a fun gimmick. 'A hundred dollars and not a cent more.'

" 'Well,' the salesman said, seemingly unaware of what he had said with the cloak on, 'I couldn't possibly accept such a low offer.'

"Zack started to put the cloak back across the trunk where he had found it. 'Not a cent more.'

" 'Okay. You win. You drive a hard bargain, sir.'

"As Zack left the shop with the cloak in a box under his arm, he glanced at his watch. 'Shit' he muttered. 'If I don't hustle my buns I'm going to be late.' He broke into a trot and arrived at a small neighborhood restaurant at exactly one o'clock. His girlfriend, Shelly, was waiting, looking particularly lovely in a soft blue wool dress. 'I'm sorry I'm late,' Zack said when they were seated at a small table. 'I got to browsing in that new antique store a few blocks east and I lost track of time.' He placed the box on his lap.

"Staring at it, Shelly said, 'Oh, wonderful. You did remember. I was sure you wouldn't.' Her blue eyes were bright with anticipation, her white teeth revealed by her wide grin.

"Remember? Shit, Zack thought. Her birthday. I forgot completely. Zack and Shelly had been going together for more than five months and he was really fond of her. He felt the box resting on his thighs. The cloak. You know, he thought, I'd rather be lucky than good any day. 'Of course I remembered,' he said, lifting the box. 'That's why I was late. I looked and looked for just the right thing. I fell in love with this and I hope you like it.' He handed her the box and she opened it and gazed at the contents.

" 'Oh, Zack. It's beautiful,' she said, fingering the soft fabric. 'It looks like something someone would have worn hundreds of years ago.' She leaned across the table and gave him a small kiss on the lips. 'No other man would have thought to buy a woman clothing, and this is just perfect. Can I put it on right now?'

"Phew. Even if the veracity part was a gimmick, she liked the cloak. 'Sure. I'd love to see how you look.'

"Shelly stood and carefully placed the cloak over her

shoulders. 'Zack, it's wonderful.' She sat back down, the cloak still around her.

" 'Would you like to order?' Zack asked.

"Shelly gazed at Zack, a glint in her eyes. 'I'd really prefer to go back to your place and celebrate my birthday privately.'

"He had never expected an answer like that. Shelly enjoyed their occasional lunches out and never made leading suggestions like the one she had just made. 'Really? Don't you have to be back at work?'

" 'Mr. McAllister is away and I really have nothing to do. I'll call them and tell them I'm taking my birthday afternoon off. Then we can spend it together.'

" 'Wow. That would be great.' He stood. 'Let's get out of here.'

"Shelly called her office and made her excuses, then they chatted on the short walk to his building and up in the elevator. Although Shelly was a bit more outspoken than usual, Zack didn't think much of it. As he closed the apartment door behind them, he asked, 'Would you like something to eat? We didn't get lunch after all. I could see what's in the kitchen.'

" 'I don't want to eat,' she said softly. 'I just want you.'

"Zack stood stock-still. Never had Shelly behaved as she was now. Could it be the cloak? Was she being forced to tell the absolute truth? 'You want me? For what?'

"Shelly ducked her head. 'I just love your body. It makes me hungry just looking at you but it really embarrasses me to say it.'

" 'Let's go inside,' Zack said, leading Shelly into the bedroom. 'We can talk about this.' As she sat down on the edge of the bed, her soft skirt slid up her smooth white thighs. She pulled her skirt down just a bit and clasped her hands primly in her lap.

" 'Now, tell me,' he said, 'what would you like me to do now?'

"Shelly's gaze fastened on Zack's. 'I would like you to touch me.'

"Zack crouched at her feet and placed one hand on her knee. Her stockings felt slithery beneath his palm. Slowly he slid his hand to the inside of her thigh, working his fingers slowly upward. 'Does that feel good?' he asked.

" 'Oh yes,' she purred. 'Very good.'

" 'Then spread your legs slightly so I can touch you better,' Zack said softly and was surprised when she did as he asked. He eased his fingers to the top of her stockings and found the soft, incredibly warm skin above. He kept his fingers moving, occasionally brushing the crotch of her silky panties.

" 'Maybe we should take off some of these clothes,' Shelly said.

"Not the cloak, he thought. She stood and dropped the cloak onto the bed, then pulled her dress off over her head and stood before him wearing only her undies, garter belt, and hose. He quickly removed his clothes until he was wearing only his briefs. 'Aren't you cold?' Zack asked. 'Let me wrap this cloak around you.' Before she could get her bearings he swirled the cloak around her near-naked shoulders. 'That should keep you warm.'

" 'I'd rather you kept me warm,' she said, moving closer, pressing her satin-covered breasts against his chest, raising her face for a kiss.

"Zack pressed his mouth against hers, softly at first.

*Then, encouraged by her enthusiasm, he wrapped his
arms around her and, as she opened her mouth, he
pressed his tongue inside. For long minutes they played,
tongue to tongue, her hands sliding up his chest to
tangle in his hair.*

" '*What would you like now?*' *he asked.*

" '*Undress the rest of me,*' *she said without hesitation,
'and kiss everything you uncover.*'

"*Her bra went first. Zack loved her beautiful breasts
and eagerly kissed and suckled their tempting, erect nipples. He drew first one bud then the other into his
mouth, sucking and nipping until he could hear Shelly's
rasping breath. 'More,' she groaned.*

"*He knelt at her feet and slowly pulled her silky panties down to her ankles, lifting each foot so she could
step out. 'Spread your legs a bit,' he said hoarsely. When
her legs parted, he eased his fingers through her pussy
hair to her hot, wet center. She was soaking, dripping
love juices and trembling. He knew she wanted to lie
down, but he kept her standing, caressing all the tender
places usually so carefully hidden.*

"*Finally, when he thought she could take no more,
he lowered her to the bed, the cloak still partially
around her. His erection was so large, it was almost
painful, but he wanted to hear her ask for him. 'What
now?'*

" '*I want you inside of me. Fill me up. Please.*'

" '*Maybe this way.*' *He pressed first one, then two
fingers inside her, pushing, then withdrawing in mock
intercourse. He sucked at her white breasts while he
finger-fucked her pussy.*

" '*Baby, fuck me. Please. I want to feel your cock
inside of me.*'

"*Never had she used such language, and it aroused*

him still further. 'Right now, baby,' Zack said. 'Right now.' He quickly put on a condom then touched the tip of his cock to her heat and slowly pushed inside. It obviously wasn't fast enough for her and he felt her fingernails on his buttocks, urging him deeper. Still he held back, waiting until she was thrashing and squirming. Then she wrapped her legs around his waist and drove her hips upward until he was lodged totally within her.

"He could feel small tremors in her channel, then a tight squeezing. 'Oh, baby,' he moaned, unable to resist any longer. He pulled back, then plunged, over and over until, with a scream she came. Only moments later his orgasm mimicked hers.

"Later he rolled onto his back and Shelly snuggled against his side, her head on his shoulder. 'Wow,' she said. 'I don't know what came over me, but that was amazing.'

" 'Yes, it certainly was.' He shuddered.

" 'You're chilly. Let me just put this over you.' She draped the cloak over the two of them. 'Was this lovemaking okay?'

" 'Okay?' he said, unable and unwilling to deny anything, 'it was the best ever.'

" 'Is there any way I could make it better?'

"Zack felt his cock stir. 'Not better, just more. And there are so many ways.' He tucked the cloak around the two of them, knowing he would be incapable of telling anything but the truth about their lovemaking, and delighted at the prospect."

Ellen found the stop button on the CD player by touch in the darkened room and pressed it. She felt the distance between her body and Jim's. "I'm sorry. Did that story turn you off?" she asked as the silence dragged on.

"Oh no," Jim said. "I'm a bit overwhelmed. I never realized that others had the same doubts, the same insecurities, and the same desire to know what to do. The author of the story must have known, however, because he hit the nail right on the head."

"What if you had a cloak like that right now?" Ellen whispered. "Would you throw it around my shoulders?" Would she be brave enough to tell him what she wanted? Well, she thought, she'd gotten herself into this and she really wanted to make love with Jim. Now! Yet she wouldn't rush him.

Jim took her hand in his and she could feel the trembling. "We're not going too fast?" he asked.

"I find you very attractive and I think we'd have fun together. It just seems a natural way to go."

Jim took another deep breath and asked, "If I threw the cloak over your shoulders, what would you say?"

"I'd say that I'd like you to kiss me."

Chapter 12

In the dimly lit room, their mouths came together. Jim's lips were soft and warm, tentative yet firm. Ellen felt her body melt against him as his arms wound around her shoulders. His tongue slipped between her lips and their heads naturally moved to deepen the kiss. He threaded his fingers through her hair and she rested her palms on his shoulders. "Oh, sweet," he murmured, moving his mouth against hers.

"God," Ellen said, separating for a moment. It was obvious that the story had done more than facilitate communication. It had turned him on. "You take my breath away. You're a fantastic kisser." In one small part of her mind she thought about Kevin. He was a sensitive lover, but he wasn't particularly into kissing. Shy and a bit hesitant as Jim was, he had a terrific mouth.

"Like your friend said, maybe it's just that we're good together." His mouth again fused with hers, fueling the fire in her belly. For long minutes they kissed while his hands caressed her back and hers grasped the front of his shirt. The world faded and there was nothing but the two of them. She threw her head back as Jim's lips moved along her jaw and down the side of her neck. "You make me feel brave," he whispered. "If you were wearing that cloak now, what would you say?"

She'd gotten herself into this, she owed him honesty. She took his hand and placed it on her aching breast. Her nipple was hard, almost painfully contracted and she needed his touch. "I want you here."

"Oh, Ellen," he moaned, filling his palm with her flesh.

She fell back against the sofa and pressed against his hand, reveling in the feel of his fingers kneading her breast. "You make me so hungry." She unbuttoned her blouse and urged his hand inside.

He touched the cup of her bra and slid his fingers beneath the lace, finding her pebbled tip. "Tell me," he growled.

"Pinch it. Make me feel you." He did and it caused bolts of molten heat to stab through her. "More," she groaned.

In one motion Jim grabbed the front of her blouse and pulled it from her skirt, popping one of the buttons in his haste. He quickly dragged it from her shoulders and, in one motion unfastened her bra and yanked it off, tossing both across the room. "Now what?" he asked, more a demand for an answer than a question.

Ellen felt the cool air against her burning skin. "Your mouth," she moaned. She cupped her breast. "Here."

"I want to see you," he said, fumbling for the light and turning it on. "Oh, God, I knew you'd be beautiful." He dropped his head and his mouth found her turgid nipple, drawing it inside.

She was barely able to think, but in some far-away part of her brain she realized that she was as excited as she had been with Kevin. Different. Not better, just different. Different. As she cupped her palms against the sides of Jim's head and held him close, his lips did magical things to her breast. Then his fingers found her other nipple and she was no longer capable of thinking anything.

Without conscious thought, her fingers unbuttoned his shirt and yanked it off. "I want to feel your skin against mine."

He held her, his mouth playing music on her lips, his chest hair rubbing against her wet nipples. Textures. It was all textures. His chest hair tickled her, his fingernails scratched her back, his soft lips nibbled at her mouth. Then he sat back, his eyes glazed. "The cloak is still around your shoulders," he said, his voice rough. "Tell me, what now?"

"I want to see all of you. I want you to undress me, too. Let's go inside."

She led him into her small bedroom and turned on the light. In one motion she pulled the covers off the bed and dumped them to the floor. She stood at the bottom of the bed, legs slightly spread. He knelt at her feet as he pulled off her shoes, lifting first one foot then the other. As he fumbled with her garters, he said, "I can't get my fingers to work."

Quickly she pulled off her skirt and unhooked the garters. She dropped her hands at her sides as he slowly peeled the nylons down her legs. He pressed his face against the tops of her thighs and kissed the soft white skin there, allowing his breath to heat her. He rubbed his long mustache over her belly and she couldn't decide whether it tickled or just drove her crazy. As he kissed her mound through her panties, he cupped her buttocks to hold her close.

Ellen gently drew him up. "Now you," she said. Marveling at the mat of sandy hair that covered his chest, she ran her fingers through the soft fur, then over his male nipples as he trembled beneath her palms. Unable to control her own body enough to crouch, she sat on the floor and tugged off his shoes and socks, then she slid her hands up the front of his pants, stroking the large bulge with her thumbs. She unbuttoned his slacks and lifted herself to her knees. "I've always wanted to do this," she whispered, grasping the tab of the zipper in her teeth. Slowly, inexorably, the zipper opened. She remembered how good his breath had felt so, as the top of his pants parted, she blew on the opening of his shorts and smiled as she felt him shudder.

His hands lifted her and together they lay down on the bed. He moved so they were head-to-foot and his mouth found her mound through her panties. His heat and the magic of his mouth made her crazy with need, but she restrained the urge to rip off clothing and drag him inside of her. Instead she covered her teeth with her lips and bit him through his shorts.

"Damn, woman," he growled, "if you do that I won't last worth a damn."

"Who wants you to last?" she asked.

"You've still got the cloak on," he whispered.

"Fuck me," she told him. "I want you inside of me. Now!"

He yanked off his shorts and her panties and climbed off the bed. She watched as he found a condom in his pants pocket and opened the foil. "Let me do that," she said.

Taking the rolled latex, she held it against the tip of his penis and slowly—agonizingly slowly—unrolled it over him. "You said 'Now!' if I recall."

Ellen giggled. "So I lied."

"You can't lie with the cloak around your shoulders."

She held his cock in her hand as he knelt over her. Raising her hips, she said, "Yes. Now! Do it!"

He needed no help finding the center of her wet pussy and he plunged inside. Over and over he thrust, then found her clit with his fingers between their bodies. He angled his pelvis so he could piston into her while rubbing her nub with his thumb. "God, baby, so good," he gasped.

"So good," she echoed as she climbed to the ultimate heights. She grabbed his ass cheeks and held him tightly against her as he came, then she joined him, the power and rhythm of his pounding pushing her over the edge.

They lay together dozing for quite a while, until finally Ellen asked, "Is that cloak still around my shoulders?"

"Of course," Jim said.

With a wicked grin she admitted, "I'm hungry. Let's get dinner, then come back here later and see what develops."

Laughter coloring his voice, he said, "Done. I like the way you think."

"Way to go, Ellen!" Lucy cried, pumping her fist in the air. "I knew she had it in her. Seducing a man isn't an easy task. She's certainly becoming my kind of woman."

"Lucy," Maggie said, appearing on a chair in the computer room. "You promised not to watch."

"She won't know, and I only watched for a few moments."

"Lucy," Angie said, "you didn't."

Looking not the least bit contrite, Lucy said, "Let's just say the devil made me do it."

"Right," the two other women said.

"So it seems Ellen's becoming a sexual being," Maggie said. "What's left for me to do?"

"She has to become a complete woman. She has to understand her power and her responsibility," Angie said, "especially with all that money."

"Hey, who said anything about that?" Lucy argued. "All I wanted was for her to learn to fuck like a bunny."

"That's not enough, Luce," Angela said. "She's learned a

little about sex, thanks to Maggie here, but there's more to real life than casual sex."

"You're not talking about marriage and all that traditional claptrap, are you, love?" Lucy's tail twitched.

"No, not really. Now that she's stuck her head out of her cocoon, she's got to figure out where she fits. She's got to leave the nest and make her place in the world."

Maggie sat forward in her chair. "That's a bit out of my league. Am I supposed to teach her that, too? Me, who spent most of her life enjoying the hell out of casual sex? I think you've got the wrong woman for this part of the job."

"Not at all," Angela protested. "You weren't married for most of your adult life but you know where you fit. You gave pleasure, taught men about themselves, and saved many a marriage with your wisdom."

"Come on, Angela," Maggie said, "I was just a hooker."

"If you had been *just* a hooker you wouldn't be here. It's the good you did that keeps you in limbo here with us."

"So what am I supposed to do now?"

"Just be there when the time comes to help her understand where she's going. Not a specific destination, just a direction. She has none right now."

"I'm not sure I know what you mean."

"You will. Just be yourself and you'll know what to say when the need arises. It will be a while, but the moment will come."

Maggie shook her head. "If you say so, ladies."

"We do," the two women said together.

As Maggie disappeared from the computer room, Lucy looked at Angela. "We do?"

"We do." Angela's wings quivered as the two returned to their computer screens.

*   *   *

It was wonderful for Ellen to watch the way Jim changed over the following weeks. They dated at least twice a week and their lovemaking became freer and more creative, with Jim taking the lead as often as Ellen did. He laughed during sex and made suggestions about fantasies he'd like to act out. One evening he suggested that they listen to a random story on the CD and do whatever the characters in the tale enjoyed.

Ellen giggled. "I know all the stories by heart by now," she said, "so it would be unfair for me to pick one. They progress from the traditional to the, well let's say kinky. Why don't you pick a number from one to eight?"

The twinkle in Jim's eye was obvious. "You know, before I met you I would have picked one or two. Now, let's see what number eight has to say."

Ellen hesitated, knowing the theme of that story. "You're in for quite a surprise," she said, pressing the play button.

"Is there magic in the world? Skeptics doubt that magic exists, or ever did exist. Are they right? I don't know, but there are still a few people who are willing to keep an open mind, people who believe in old stories, ancient legends, and possibilities. Like the possibilities inherent in the Wand of Forgetfulness.

" 'Look out!' Phil, among others, shouted as the old woman started to cross the street. A taxi, careening around the corner, was heading straight for her.

"The woman looked around, seemingly dazed by the shouting, still standing directly in the path of the speeding vehicle. 'Look out, lady!' Phil shouted again but the woman seemed frozen, unable to take the two steps that would move her out of harm's way. No way around it, Phil thought. He leaped out into the street, grabbed the

slight woman by the shoulders and dragged her onto the sidewalk just as the taxi roared past, the driver making obscene hand gestures.

" 'Goodness, young man,' the woman said, her hand placed against the center of her chest, her breathing ragged. Trembling, she continued, 'I heard you call, and saw the car but I couldn't seem to move.' She grasped Phil's arm trying not to collapse.

" 'It's okay now,' Phil said. 'You're safe and none worse for the wear.'

" 'Thanks to you.' She placed her hand flat on her chest again and took several deep breaths. 'My goodness I'm all fluttery. I can't thank you enough.'

" 'I didn't do anything special,' he said. 'I just did what had to be done. Lots of other people would have done the same.'

" 'But they didn't and you did. You were very brave and you deserve a reward.'

"Phil stared at the woman's unkempt appearance. She seemed one step up from a bag lady, her clothes worn, patched, and many times washed, her straggly hair caught under a faded brown bandanna. 'It's nothing. Please don't think about it anymore.' He started to move toward the bus stop.

" 'I know you're probably running late, but let me do what I want. It's not nice to argue with an old lady.' She rummaged in the large shopping bag that hung from one skinny wrist. 'Here's what I'm looking for,' she exclaimed, withdrawing a slender box about a foot long and no larger around than a quarter. Pressing it into Phil's hand, she said, 'This is the Wand of Forgetfulness. If you touch someone on the shoulder with this, he or she will forget whatever you've done for the past *hour or so. You could rob banks, tell your boss off, whatever. It's of no use to me now and I do so want you to have it.'*

"*Phil tried not to take the box but the woman persisted. 'Please. Humor an old lady,' she said, holding Phil's hand closed around the box.*

"*Realizing that it was easier to just take the silly thing than to argue, he shoved the package into his briefcase. 'Thanks, ma'am,' he said.*

"*The woman patted him on the shoulder. 'Use it wisely. Oh, and you can only use it three times. Then you have to give it away.'*

" *'Sure. That's wonderful. Thanks. Really. I appreciate it. Now I've got to catch my bus.'*

" *'Of course. You're my hero, young man, and thank you again for saving my life.'*

"*Phil thought little about the slender box in his briefcase as he rode the bus home. After a dinner of Kentucky Fried Chicken with his wife, Kate, and their two children, he played with the kids while Kate finished up some business she'd brought home. After the children were in bed, Phil and Kate sat in the living room holding hands.*

"*As he relaxed, Phil told Kate about the strange woman who had given him the Wand of Forgetfulness. 'That's really silly,' Kate said, looking at the box in Phil's hand. 'I can't believe she actually told you that. Do you think she believed it?'*

" *'She seemed to believe every word of what she told me.' He opened the box and withdrew a slender ebony rod with silver tips on each end. 'It looks like one of those batons conductors use.' He stood up and waved the stick in the air as if leading an orchestra. 'I think it makes me look very distinguished.'*

" 'You look silly,' Kate said, grinning, 'but awful cute.'

"As he sat down, Phil tapped Kate on the shoulder with the wand. Kate looked a bit confused, then said, 'What's that thing?'

" 'What thing?'

" 'That stick. It looks like the thing conductors use with orchestras.'

"Totally puzzled, Phil said, 'This is the wand the old woman gave me.'

" 'What old woman?' Kate asked.

" 'Nothing,' Phil said, shaking his head. He dropped back onto the sofa. She had completely forgotten what he had just told her. Could what the old woman said be true? Did the wand really work? He had to think about it then maybe test it out. But he only had three cracks at it and he'd already used one. Stop it, he told himself. You're starting to sound like you believe this junk.

"Phil thought of little else for several days and finally decided to give the wand another chance. He called his secretary into his office, gave her a list of meaningless tasks, then touched her on the shoulder with the wand. She remembered nothing of what he had just said. Amazed he dismissed the baffled woman and dropped into his desk chair. It had actually worked, and he had one more opportunity to use it. What would he do?

"Rob a bank? Not a chance. He wasn't that kind of person. Tell his boss off? Why waste his final shot? No, he would have to wait and continue to ponder. There would be a right moment and he'd be ready.

"Several weeks later, Kate and Phil sent the children to Kate's parents overnight so they could attend a party with Kate's boss and several important clients. Kate *chose to wear an incredibly sexy teal-blue dress that was so tiny that as they stood around a table of hors d'oeuvres Phil saw several men gaze longingly at his wife's neckline and great legs. Not that she flirted or gave them any encouragement, of course. He just had one hell of a sexy wife.*

"*As he gazed at her, he focused on the amazingly erotic nape of her neck. He had always found that spot an incredible turn-on and the way she was wearing her hair, pinned up in a tight twist, just accentuated it. All Phil could think about was kissing and biting that deliciously tasty spot and the one where her neck joined her shoulder. He pictured himself ripping the dress off her body, tying her to the bed then kissing and fucking her senseless. He moved to ease the pressure in his suit pants. Tying her to the bed.*

"She'd never go for it, *he thought.* Not his sweet little wife, mother of his children, but hell he was hungry. He just wanted to throw her down and take her, eat her alive then fuck her brains out. He began to think about the Wand of Forgetfulness. He could do anything he wanted, then just tap her on the shoulder and she'd forget. He could really do it.

"*Suddenly the bulge in his pants grew to still more uncomfortable proportions.* I can do whatever I want, then just tap her and she'll forget. I can have the best sex ever and it would fuel fantasies forever. *He sighed and slipped a hand into his pants pocket so he could adjust his cock more comfortably in the front of his jockey shorts.* How am I going to last until we can leave? *he wondered. The evening dragged but he made it through, thinking and planning, deciding exactly what he was going to do, and how. He had it all figured out by the time they arrived back at their house.*

" 'That was a really nice evening,' Kate said, yawning. 'I'm beat.'

" 'Let's go upstairs,' Phil said, guiding his wife up to their bedroom. When he had closed the door behind them, he ordered, 'Take that dress off.'

"Kate looked at him a bit startled. When she didn't move quickly enough Phil said, 'Take it off. Now! Unless you want it ripped off your body.'

"Kate stared, then giggled and said, 'I love you when you're masterful.' She slithered out of the dress and stood there dressed in a silk slip, a slight grin on her face.

" 'You won't be smiling long,' Phil snapped. 'Get over here.' God it felt good, giving instructions. And when it was all over he'd just make her forget.

"Slowly Kate walked over looking a bit puzzled. 'Baby, what's gotten into you?'

" 'I just want to fuck your sweet body.' He grabbed her wrists and pulled them behind her, holding both in one large hand. He grabbed the back of her head with the other and buried his face in the soft skin of her neck. He nibbled, then bit her, not strongly enough to cause real pain, just enough to make her body stiffen. He devoured her shoulders, then nipped his way up to her ear. He sucked the lobe into his mouth and used his teeth until he felt her breathing quicken. He turned her around and, still holding her wrists, he licked and bit the nape of her neck for several long minutes.

"When he had kissed and licked and nibbled as much as he wanted, he pushed her onto the bed. He had thought it all through so without giving her a chance to react, he quickly grabbed two of his ties and fastened Kate's hands to the headboard. He watched as she squirmed, admiring what her writhing did to her breasts as they pressed against the satiny fabric of her slip. 'Baby, what's this all about?' she hissed.

" 'I want you. This way. My way. And you can't do anything about it.' He watched her start to speak, then close her mouth. 'Good girl. You have no say in this.' When she remained silent, he continued, 'Good. I see you understand. Now, I hope you're not wearing panty hose.' He yanked off her shoes and, finding stockings and garters, he unfastened one stocking and dragged it down her leg. Then he used it to tie her ankle to the footboard. He quickly did the same to her other leg.

"Now he took several minutes to admire his deliciously sexy wife, tied spread-eagle to the bed, ready for whatever he wanted to do. Where to begin? From the bathroom he got a large pair of shears. He sat beside his still-silent wife, snapping the shears loudly, then, without a word, he began to cut the slip up the front. 'I've dreamed of doing this forever.' When he reached the top, he spread the slip's sides and gazed at the tiny wisp of lace that held her breasts. 'So beautiful,' he whispered.

"He leaned over and used his teeth on her already erect nipple, biting hard so she'd feel it through the material. Then he bit the other. Back and forth he moved until the cups of her bra were wet and he could see her dark areolas and the large protruding tips. Then he cut through the front of the bra and parted the cups so he could admire his wife's naked breasts. No, he thought, not breasts, tits. Creamy, white tits. 'You've got great tits,' he said, amazed that he could use such a word in front of his prim little wife. But he'd make her forget it all later.

"Kissing her full on the mouth, he felt her tongue reach for his. God, he was hot. He snipped through *shoulder straps and pulled both slip and bra out from beneath her. Then he cut the garter belt and the sides of her panties. 'You've also got a beautiful bush. I can't wait to fuck your sweet pussy.' He could say the things he'd always wanted to growl at her while they made love.*

"He looked at her face momentarily and saw her wide eyes, her slightly bruised mouth. *'Sexy as hell,'* he said, *his voice harsh. 'You make my cock so hard I could almost come in my pants.' He reached between Kate's legs and fingered her slit, her legs unable to close, her body unable to avoid him. She was dripping wet, squirming against his hands. He stabbed his thumb into her. 'No, I'm not going to come in my pants. I'm going to come in your sweet pussy. I'm going to fuck you hard and fast, just the way I want.'*

"Quickly Phil dragged off his slacks, shirt, and underwear. His cock was so hard it was almost painful. He stretched out on top of his wife, running his hands all over her now-naked body. He rubbed his scratchy cheek on her belly, pinched her nipples, scraped his nails down her sides. Then, when he couldn't wait another minute, he plunged deep inside of her, ramming his cock into her pussy over and over, not caring about her pleasure, only his own. 'Such a hot little snatch. So tight. So wet. God so good,' he moaned. 'God! Shit!' He came almost too quickly, thrusting his cock into Kate's body.

"Later, after he caught his breath, he rolled off her and untied her wrists and ankles. 'Damn. It happened too fast, and I only had one chance.'

"Kate opened her eyes and stared at her husband. 'What do you mean only one chance?'

"He got the slim ebony wand from his dresser drawer. 'You've forgotten the story, but I already told you what this is and how I got it.' He told her the story again,* *and included his tap on her shoulder and his secretary's forgetting his errands. 'So that's the story. I've wanted to fuck you like that for years, but I knew you'd never go for it. So now I can tap you with this wand and you won't remember.'*

" 'Why in hell would you do that?' Her eyes were wide and shining.

" 'Excuse me?'

" 'Why would you want me to forget the best sex I've ever had?'

" 'You mean you enjoyed it?'

" 'You mean you couldn't tell?'

"As Phil thought back he realized that she had been extraordinarily wet. She'd been thrashing around on the bed, as much as she could while tied, moaning and calling his name. He'd been so wrapped up with his own pleasure that he hadn't been aware of hers. He felt stupefied.

" 'I probably wouldn't have gone for it if you'd given me a choice, but once you tied me up, I was incredibly excited. And those words you said, you know, the dirty ones, made me so hot. I must have climaxed a dozen times.'

"Phil's mind was reeling. 'Really?'

"Kate grinned and kissed her husband. 'I wouldn't have believed it myself. Don't you dare use that wand on me. I want to remember this until we get the chance to do it again. We can, can't we?'

"Phil put the wand on the bedside table. 'Oh, Kate, I never knew. I've fantasized about a night like this for years. I just never had the nerve to try it.'

" 'You did now, and it wasn't perfect. You came too fast, after all. I guess we'll just have to practice. I won-

der whether we can get my parents to take the kids next Saturday night.'

" 'If not, I'll bet mine will. I'll see to it.' Phil snuggled against his wife. The Wand of Forgetfulness had turned out to be a godsend. Thanks, lady, he thought. Thanks a lot."

CHAPTER 13

"Phew," Jim said. "That was some pretty heavy stuff. Have you ever done anything like that? Been tied up I mean? Do you think it would turn you on?"

Ellen was trembling. She had known, of course, what the story entailed, but she had never considered listening to that story with a man, much less telling anyone how it made her feel. They had always been honest with each other, however, a quality she treasured. "I've never done it, but the idea of it makes me crazy."

Jim turned her shoulders and cupped her chin so she had to look him in the eye. "Good crazy?"

"I have always been honest with you so yes, good crazy."

"I was hoping you'd say that." As he continued, he looked a bit chagrined. "We have always been honest with each other so I have a confession to make. I've listened to all the stories on the CD before. I knew what number eight was about, and this was my way of asking whether you'd be interested. You're not the only one who thought about using the stories for communication." Ellen just stared at him as he continued, "I couldn't ask you right out so I thought up this way to find out whether you'd be interested in playing."

"You planned this?"

He held his hands up, palms out. "I confess. I've been playing the CD whenever I get the chance. Last weekend, while you were in the shower, I finally listened to that last story and the picture of you, tied to your bed has been driving me nuts ever since." He draped his arm around her shoulder. "I couldn't think of how to tell you, so I . . . well."

Ellen took a deep breath. How far they had come. Two people, both unsure of their own sexuality, now able to discuss something so intimate, so scary, so kinky. With a gleam in her eye, she asked, "You wouldn't actually do something like that, would you?"

Jim stared at her for a long time. She winked. "Would you?" He smiled, nodded, then grabbed her wrist and pulled her to a standing position. "Yes, I would." He all but dragged her into the bedroom, pushed her down onto the bed, then growled, "Stay right there." He disappeared into the living room and returned a moment later.

Silent, Ellen stared at the plastic shopping bag he'd been carrying when he arrived. As she started to sit up he snapped, "Don't move."

"I'm sorry," she said, easily slipping into a submissive role.

"Good. Now, I'll bet you're curious about what's in this bag. Actually I got really daring on my way over here. We've passed that adult toy store on the next block several times and I've been tempted to go in. This afternoon, I did, and I bought a few items."

"You actually went in?" Ellen asked. "I've been tempted so many times, but I've never had the courage."

"Be still, woman," Jim said. "I'm the boss here tonight."

Ellen lay back on the bed and grinned. This was so great and he was so wonderful. He had changed so much since their first evening together, confidence growing week by week. He sat beside her and asked, "You trust me, don't you?"

"Totally."

His face lit up as he stood up. "Strip."

Silently, Ellen removed all her clothes and lay back on the bed while Jim rummaged in the bag and pulled out several leather straps. "I've been dreaming about this since I first heard that story." He gazed appreciatively at Ellen's naked body, then buckled the straps around wrists. "I surfed the Net looking at pictures of women tied up and I got some great ideas. The store gave me more."

He pulled a belt with rings and chains attached all around from the bag and fastened it tightly around her waist. He snapped the ring on one wristband to the end of a short piece of chain with a small padlock, then ran the chain through a ring at the front of her belt. Another padlock connected the chain to her other wrist. "You know," he said, slipping out of character, "I never would have imagined that I'd have the nerve to do this, but with you anything's possible."

From the bag he took two more straps and fastened them to Ellen's ankles, forced her to bend her knees then clipped the ankle straps to chains on the belt so her heels almost touched her buttocks and her legs fell open. He ran his finger through her slippery pussy. "You're so wet. This makes you as excited as it makes me, doesn't it?" When she didn't answer, he raised his voice. "Doesn't it?"

Ellen couldn't think. She was helpless, forced into a most revealing position, her body displayed and wide open for him. And she was so incredibly turned on. "Yes," she said, her voice ragged. "Oh, God, yes."

"Good."

Still fully clothed, Jim put the bag on the side of the bed. "Now the fun part." He withdrew a large flesh-colored dildo from the bag and held it where Ellen could see. "I've never played with toys before, but you make me feel daring." He slid the tip of the plastic phallus through her soaked folds, then slowly pushed it into her body.

Ellen's hips bucked as she tried to fuck the dildo, but Jim held it immobile deep inside of her. "Don't be in such a hurry," he purred. "We've got all night."

"Please," Ellen begged, "you're teasing me, driving me crazy. Please."

"Please what?"

"Shit," she hissed. "Get those clothes off and fuck me."

Jim grinned. "Nope. Not just yet." He pulled the dildo out slowly, then pushed it back in. In a slow-motion imitation of thrusting, he teased and tempted, never letting her have what she so desperately needed. Finally he pulled a chain from the bag, threaded it through the ring on the base of the dildo, clipping it to the back of the belt, then to the front. Now the dildo was tightly imbedded, unmoving in Ellen's pussy.

Her muscles grasped the dildo, squeezing, trying to make still more intimate contact. She moved her hips but the phallus remained still. "Oh, baby, please," she moaned, almost incoherent.

Jim only smiled, then knelt on the floor beside the bed. He brushed his mustache over her erect nipples, then nibbled on the tips. He licked and bit the flesh on her sides, her belly, her thighs as she moaned and begged him to fuck her. Then he said, "I'll bet I can make you come with just one touch." He reached between her spread legs and tapped on her clit.

Her orgasm was explosive, the power of it almost overwhelming her. When she collapsed, replete, Jim moved the dildo inside of her and she was back as high as she had been before her climax. How was that possible? She didn't know and didn't care. Over and over he teased orgasms out of her until she was totally exhausted. Then he stripped and stood beside her, grasped a handful of her hair and forced her head back. He held his erect cock and growled, "Open your mouth."

She had performed oral sex on him several times before but this was different, more elemental, primitive. He had never come in her mouth, but tonight it was as though it was preordained that she would swallow every bit of his come. She opened her mouth and he rammed his cock inside. She sucked, licked, and nipped at him until, with a long groan, he came, spurting in her throat.

Later, they showered together in her tiny bathroom. As he washed her mound he said, softly, "Was that all right? What I did, I mean?"

"Couldn't you tell? It was wonderful, explosive. It must have registered on seismographs from here to Alaska." She took the soap from him, lathered her hands, and cupped his testicles and flaccid penis in her hands.

"I don't think I'm going to be ready for sex again for a week," he said as she massaged him.

"I wouldn't bet the farm on that," she said. As she rubbed, his cock stiffened.

"You're a witch," he said. "I want to fuck you again right here but the condoms are in the bedroom."

"Don't worry about that," she said, rubbing his cock. "I don't think I'm up to another round, so I guess you'd better just fuck my hand."

"What?"

Water pouring over her head, she snapped, "Do it. Now!"

She filled the palm of her hand with shampoo and made a tube of her fingers. Jim rammed his cock through and came quickly.

Later, stretched out on the bed together, he asked, "What are you doing for the holidays? I'd love to spend the millennium celebration with you."

"I'm leaving for Fairmont in the morning," she said. When had she decided that? she wondered, but she knew when she said it that it was the right thing to do. She wanted to see how the town would feel to her now that she'd been in the city for these past months. She also wanted to visit with Micki and her family and needed to do some thinking. "I don't know when I'll be back exactly."

She felt Jim's body tighten. "It's not because of what we did tonight, is it? You are coming back, aren't you?"

She turned and put her arms around him. "I loved what we did tonight and I'll definitely be back." She slapped him on the hip. "Now it's time for you to be getting home."

He sat up slowly. "Maybe I could stay over?" he said softly.

"Not tonight. I need to do some thinking about me and where my life is going. I don't understand my future just yet."

"I hope I'll be part of your future." She could see the fear and doubts in the slump of his shoulders as he sat on the edge of the bed.

"You are, of course, but so many other things impact it too. I've never made any secret about the fact that I've been with another guy often since before I met you."

"I know, and that's the agreement we've had—no strings and no commitments. It bothers me, but I understand that you need your space."

Ellen leaned forward and kissed Jim's back. "I do. That's part of what I need to think through, away from you and him. Casual sex isn't life for me. It's sort of treading water. I need to find a direction."

"If casual sex isn't for you, we could get married, make it a full-time, permanent thing."

"That's not a reason to get married and we're not ready yet. I'm not sure what I'm ready for, but let's not rush into anything. It might happen, it might not but I never want to lead you on by letting you think that I understand any of this. I need to think and I can't do it here, with you or Kevin."

"If that's what you need, I'll miss you."

She kissed him again. "I'll miss you too."

The following morning she called Kevin and told him that she would be out of town for a few weeks.

"But love, what about the final painting of you? It's almost completed. And what about your landscapes? They are coming along so well. And us?"

She noticed immediately that the painting came first. Ellen glanced around her apartment. Several sheets of heavy cardboard stood balanced against the walls with landscapes clipped to them. All the scenes were woodsy, with babbling brooks and sun-dappled glades. Her work was progressing, but none of them made her happy. Suddenly she realized that nothing made her happy deep inside. The sex was wonderful. Jim and Kevin were both great guys, but this wasn't life. Was Jim her future? "I'll see you when I get back."

"Well, if you must. Have a happy holiday. I'll miss you."

"I'll miss you, too."

She called her sister and told her that she'd be arriving the following afternoon and proceeded to pack a few things in a small suitcase. The holiday gifts she had purchased for her sister, brother-in-law, and her nieces had already been sent home. Where was home?

As Micki drove her into the small town of Fairmont, Ellen looked around. Nothing much had changed, and yet everything had. The small, unmanned firehouse looked so quiet compared with the crowds of people always hanging around in front of New York City firehouses. The Fairmont Mall boasted an eight-movie multiplex; in the city, she could see any one of a hundred movies with just a short bus ride. There was the school complex, elementary, intermediate, and high schools sharing the same now-snow-covered campus with the local community college not far away. The stores were warm and inviting, comfortable and doable. This was Fairmont, not the big city. She had been comfortable here all her life, but not anymore. As she had suspected, she no longer fit in here.

Although she had been to Fairmont for Thanksgiving, Micki's family greeted her like visiting royalty. They shared Micki's famous pot roast, with potato pancakes and applesauce, Ellen's all-time favorite meal. Since it was now only a week before Christmas, the children were wired. They didn't get to bed until after ten and by then Micki's husband was ready to settle down in the bedroom with the TV remote and "let you girls visit."

"So why the sudden visit?" Micki asked when they were comfortably seated on the sofa in her early-American living room. "We expected you on the twenty-fourth."

"It's the Christmas season and I just missed you guys."

Micki cocked her head to one side. "You never could con me, babe. What's up?"

Ellen allowed her body to slump. "I needed to figure lots of things out and one of them was Fairmont. Someone told me recently that I used the word *home* to mean here. I just wanted to know whether that was true, whether here felt like home."

"And does it?"

Ellen stretched her legs out in front of her, crossed at the ankles. "Your home feels like home and probably always will, but this town? It was where I belonged for all the years we were growing up and until I won all that money I thought that Fairmont was the only place in the world for me. That's not true anymore."

Micki sipped her coffee. "So you're moving to the city for good?"

"I think so." She sought her sister's eyes.

"Are you looking for my approval?" Micki asked.

Ellen was surprised, not only at the question but at her inability to give a snap answer. "Maybe I am."

"Well you shouldn't be." Micki set her cup on the coffee table. "I've done quite a lot of thinking over these past months. It worries me that you've always looked to me for guidance. Because I am the 'big sister,' " Micki made quote marks in the air, "we both assumed that I would know what was best, particularly after the folks died. I know what's best for me, or at least I hope I do, and I have to make decisions with Milt, for us and for the girls, but I haven't the foggiest what's best for you any more, assuming that I ever did. You're different now, more self-assured, more confident and I've been aware of that since you arrived. Listen, Ellie, it's your life. You need to make your own decisions regardless of what I think."

Ellen leaned forward and hugged her sister. "Thanks, Micki. I love you, too."

Later, Ellen reclaimed her old car from Micki's driveway and drove to the house that had been her home until recently. Micki had kept the plants watered and the rooms aired so the place was warm and inviting. As Ellen shut the door behind her, she closed her eyes and inhaled. The living room smelled of the furniture oil her mother had always used to polish the top of the upright piano, and the pine candles that had always sat on the hall table. She set her suitcase down and walked slowly into the kitchen. Cookies. Her mother had always had a teddy bear cookie jar on the counter filled with homemade Toll House or sugar cookies. Ellen wandered back toward the living room and touched the long crack in the mirror in the tiny hall, remembering when she and Micki had made it tossing a bean bag in the house despite her mother's warnings. Smiling wistfully she remembered the week that she and her sister had been grounded afterward.

Home. It was quite a concept, one she wasn't sure she understood. This house would always be her home in some ways, yet she felt as though she didn't quite belong. She thought about her little apartment in the city. Was that home? She didn't really belong there either.

And her life. What fit there? Before the lottery, she had been comfortable here. She dropped onto a kitchen chair. Comfortable. There was that word again. Was that what she should be aiming for, comfort? Did Kevin offer comfort? Did Jim? The more she thought, the more confused she became. How much of what she had always done had been settling for just comfortable and easy?

Suitcase in hand, she climbed the stairs and got ready for bed. Where was her life heading? She asked herself question after question as she slipped beneath the log-cabin–design quilt and, sighing, closed her eyes. She pictured her recent evening with Jim and the last time she'd seen Kevin. His brother, Sean, had asked again whether she would pose for him, although she knew that it was not just her posing that he was interested in. Maybe she'd let him. She found herself wondering what he'd be like coupling with her on that same velvet sofa. She closed her eyes, creating the scene.

It was mid-afternoon and the sun shown through the skylight in the studio ceiling creating an oasis of light into which Kevin pulled the sofa. He draped it in a soft blue velour and Ellen quickly removed her clothes. Kevin's totally businesslike hands positioned her on the couch, reclining, with one knee raised, her arm resting lightly across the sofa's back.

"Now," Kevin purred, turning on the radio to a classical station, "I want you to think about your lover. He's just outside the door and you can hear his key in the lock. He's been away for more than a week and you've been yearning for him to return."

Ellen formed the picture in her mind, her lover, who always looked like a cross between Kevin and Jim, about to enter the room and make love with her. She could feel her nipples tighten and her pussy swell.

"The warm sun shines on your skin," Kevin crooned, "and you can feel the heat rise in your body from both outside and within. Now the door is opening, and he comes in and kneels beside you, touching your soft belly, your full breasts, the hair between your legs."

Ellen was lost in her dream, when she heard another voice. "She's just as lovely as I imagined." Her eyes jerked open and she saw Sean at the top of the stairs. "I hope you don't mind," Sean said. "There haven't been any customers for more than an hour and I thought I'd come up and work a bit." He hadn't taken his eyes off Ellen's naked body. "Do you mind?"

Ellen thought about covering herself and realized

that she didn't really want to. Rather she reveled in the lust she saw growing in Sean's gaze. "No. I don't mind."

From one of the shelves at the side of the room, Sean pulled a cloth-covered shape and put it on a pedestal table. He removed the drape and Ellen saw that the sculpture was a standing nude that bore a distinct resemblance to her. As she watched Sean's hands stroke the surface of the clay it was as though his hands caressed her flesh. She lay, lost in the sensuality of two men's eyes devouring her nude body. As she looked from Kevin's eyes to Sean's she knew there was nothing professional about their scrutiny now.

"You know, don't you," Sean said, "that this was just an excuse to come up here and be with you." As his thumbs brushed the clay nipples Ellen's nipples became harder and tighter.

"You are so seductive, lying in the light like that," Kevin said, his voice hoarse, "that I eventually forget about painting and just want to love you."

Slowly, a smile spread over Ellen's face. "Yes," she purred.

Her one-word affirmation was all the two men needed. As one they moved beside her. Sean's hands were still wet from the statue and, as he covered her breasts with his palms, she could feel the traces of slippery clay. Kevin had brought a tube of cadmium yellow paint and squeezed a line over her ribs. Slowly four hands rubbed and stroked, covering her body with water-based sunshine.

Without ever leaving her, they were suddenly naked, too, their bodies fully ready and totally aroused. She took a tube of alizarin crimson and filled her palm. She rubbed Kevin's hard cock with the flame-red paint and skillfully manipulated his shaft. Grinning, Sean filled her other palm with cobalt paint and soon she had a hard cock in each hand.

The moans of the two men filled the studio as she brought them closer and closer to climax. It was strange that, although they were completely passive, neither touching her, she felt filled and complete. She stared at the two cocks, one blood-red and one deep blue, and rubbed, knowing exactly where each man needed to be touched. She cupped Sean's balls and slipped a finger toward Kevin's anus.

She was supremely talented, able to drive them each higher and higher. She knew that she had the power to make them come or leave them suspended over the precipice. "Now," she said, pressing Sean's sac and slowly inserting a paint-lubricated finger into Kevin's ass.

Two cocks erupted, semen mixing with color, loud roars blending with Mozart. She was the eternal woman, able to please anyone.

In her bed, Ellen touched herself and quickly climaxed and, although Ellen couldn't hear it, from far away, Lucy cheered.

The following morning, Ellen showered and walked slowly downstairs. Smelling freshly brewed coffee, she frowned as she entered the kitchen. "Maggie," she cried, rushing over to hug the older woman. "It's been forever."

"For you maybe. For me it seems like we just parted. Tell me everything that's gone on since I last saw you."

"Everything?"

Maggie picked up a plastic-coated bag and waved it beneath Ellen's nose. "I brought doughnuts. Apple-spice filled. We can eat as you talk."

Over doughnuts and coffee, Ellen filled Maggie in on her

escapades over the past weeks. Through the recitation, Maggie remained silent, content to listen to all of Ellen's tales. When Ellen finally ran down, Maggie said, "Tied you to the bed? Is this the Ellen I first met last fall, the one who didn't know about toe-curling, mind-blowing, earth-moving sex?"

"The very same—and the very different." Suddenly Ellen's eyes filled. "Oh, Maggie, I don't know where I belong anymore."

"Do you have to?" When Ellen stared, Maggie continued, "Where it is written that you have to know where you fit? Maybe the question you should be asking yourself is what makes you happy?" Maggie paused. "Here's a game I'd like you to play. Fill in the blank. *Blank* makes me happy."

"You make me happy."

"I thank you for the compliment but that's not enough. Again."

"Great sex makes me happy."

"Good. Again."

"Jim makes me happy. Kevin makes me happy."

"Again."

"Micki and her family make me happy."

"Again."

"Okay, okay, let me think."

"That's the idea of this exercise," Maggie said. "Think."

"The city makes me happy. Being on my own and making my own decisions make me happy."

"You haven't mentioned your painting."

Ellen thought. "You're right. Painting forest scenes doesn't make me happy. You know what I want to paint? Purple trees and red skies. Twin moons and black deserts."

"So paint them."

"Kevin would throw me out of class."

"So? Stop doing what you think you should, and do what gives you joy. Paint twin moons and purple trees. You said great sex makes you happy. What about love? You used to think that that would make you happy. A man and a home like Micki's."

"That's not so important now. It will come, I think, but certainly not with Kevin. He's a wonderful interlude, but nothing more than that. And Jim? He's a great guy, but despite his proposal he's not nearly ready. We know what we've got and that's enough for now. I need to find *me* before I can think about any kind of full-time, permanent relationship."

"Okay. How about your job, does that make you happy?"

"No," Ellen said quickly, "but if I don't work I'll feel like a slug. I have to do something. I can't just sit around all day painting and eating doughnuts." Saying that she reached into the bag and pulled out a second apple-spice doughnut.

"So don't. What would you like to do?"

"Months ago, when Micki and I were talking about what to do in the city, I considered volunteering in a hospital. I think I'd like to do that."

"So do it. You certainly don't need to earn money."

"That's another thing. There's all that money sitting there just earning more money."

"The problem with that is?"

"It's selfish. There are so many people who need. Not the big charities, but people. Individuals. Sick kids and pregnant teens. Children who need to learn how to read."

"Do something about it. You can, you know."

"I could start a foundation with some of that money. Or just give it away to people who need it." She took a big bite of her doughnut and, with her mouth full, continued, "I wouldn't know how to go about any of that."

"There must be people who do and I'm sure with a little searching you could find someone to help you."

"I don't want to get all serious and give up sex and fun."

"You can do everything. You have nothing holding you down."

A familiar voice filled the room. "She's right, you know."

"Lucy, are you eavesdropping again?" Maggie snapped.

"Of course we are," Angela said. "Why do you think you showed up in Ellen's kitchen on this particular morning? Ellen needed a sounding board to help her figure out this thing called life."

"Life isn't easy," Lucy chimed in. "If it were simple we wouldn't have all these 'up or down' decisions to make. Finding a path through the trees is tough."

"And there's usually no one to help you," Angela said.

"Except when you ladies send me down," Maggie said. She took Ellen's hands in hers. "Listen. You're well on your way to becoming something special, a person who has a clear idea of what makes her happy and goes after it. Don't lose that when I'm gone."

"You're leaving?"

"My job here is done." Maggie giggled. "I sound like the Lone Ranger." She lowered the pitch of her voice. "Come on, Tonto, our work here is done."

"But I'm still confused."

"You'll be confused for a long time, but you've got a direction, some ideas. The most important thing you've learned is . . . fill in the *blank*."

"Do what makes me happy, what gives me direction."

"You've got it."

Again Ellen's eyes filled. "I'm going to miss you."

"How about us?" Lucy chimed in.

"Okay," Ellen admitted, "you two also. Without all your help I don't know where I'd be."

Angela answered. "You'd be in the city, in that silly apartment, peeking out at life. Now you're experiencing it. You're flying now, babe. Soar."

Ellen grinned. "I want to get a kitten. A tiny, scrappy, female kitten. Perhaps I'll get two, a white one called Angela, and a coal-black one named Lucy."

"You're making me all misty," Angela said, a catch in her voice.

"You would get weepy," Lucy said. "I think it's cute."

Maggie stood, pulled Ellen to her feet, and wrapped her arms around her friend. "I won't be seeing you again, and if things go the way they have in the past, you'll forget me quickly."

"You've been a great friend, Maggie," Ellen said, tears running down her face.

"You have, too," Maggie said, her eyes moist. "I'm so glad I got to share this time in your life."

"Okay, you two, stop blubbering," Lucy said as her voice slowly faded. "Oh and one last thing. If you decide to keep this place, get that mirror fixed. Cracked mirrors make me crazy."

"I love you all," Ellen said as Maggie walked toward the front door.

"I love you, too," Maggie said, then opened the door and disappeared.

For a long while, Ellen stood in the center of the living room and let the tears fall. Then, when she finally calmed, she found a small pad and began to make plans for the future. Her future.

*   *   *

"So what's next for me," Maggie said, sitting in the computer room with Lucy and Angela.

"Oh, we have plenty of jobs for you." Angela swiveled her computer monitor so Maggie could see. On the screen was a tall, slender, man who looked like a twenty-first-century version of Ichabod Crane. "How would you feel about educating a man for a change? You should be really good at that."

"A man?" Maggie said. "What an idea."

Dear Reader,

I hope you've enjoyed reading *Midnight Butterfly* as much as I enjoyed writing it. I loved creating Ellen and revisiting Maggie, Lucy, and Angela from my earlier novel *Slow Dancing*, Barbara Enright's story. I have a great desire to see what happens on Maggie's next assignment and maybe I'll write that book eventually.

When I wrote *Slow Dancing*, nothing like the tape or CD collections of erotic short stories existed. Since then I've teamed up with the folks at Raven Limited to create just such CD collections, original stories that you can listen to or use for communication as Ellen and Jim did in this book. They are available through my Website at *www.JoanELloyd.com*. Please visit to learn about the CDs, read new erotic short stories I post every month, learn about and read excerpts from all my books, and share information with my thousands of visitors.

I'd love to hear from you any time, so drop me a note and let me know what you particularly enjoyed and what you would like to read about in a future book. Please write me at:

Joan E. Lloyd
PO Box 221
Yorktown Heights, NY 10598
or via e-mail at: Joan@JoanELloyd.com.